"Congratulat[...]
house," says the [...] president, Cassandra.

All the other sisters just stand and stare at me but don't say anything. It's sort of creepy.

"Here, put this on," Cassandra says, slipping a hideous purple sweatshirt on over my fabu sweater. The sweatshirt has a huge pink *Z* on the front of it.

"Oh, okay, thanks," I say, trying to be grateful, knowing that I'll rip it off the minute I'm out of their sight. The other sisters come alive as I slip into the sweatshirt and start hugging and congratulating me.

Slowly the groups file out of the Student Center to go back to their houses and celebrate. "Let's get this party started," one of the sisters says, leading the way out of the Student Center.

I smile, thinking maybe this won't be so bad after all. Maybe I will find out the sisters didn't have anything to do with Mitzi's disappearance and they will become my best friends.

"Oh, no, sweetie. Not you," Cassandra says, placing a hand on the *Z* in the middle of my sweatshirt. "This party is just for initiated sisters. You've got to earn the perks of being a Zeta."

Twisted Sisters

Stephanie Hale

BERKLEY JAM, NEW YORK

THE BERKLEY PUBLISHING GROUP
Published by the Penguin Group
Penguin Group (USA) Inc.
375 Hudson Street, New York, New York 10014, USA
Penguin Group (Canada), 90 Eglinton Avenue East, Suite 700, Toronto, Ontario M4P 2Y3, Canada
(a division of Pearson Penguin Canada Inc.)
Penguin Books Ltd., 80 Strand, London WC2R 0RL, England
Penguin Group Ireland, 25 St. Stephen's Green, Dublin 2, Ireland (a division of Penguin Books Ltd.)
Penguin Group (Australia), 250 Camberwell Road, Camberwell, Victoria 3124, Australia
(a division of Pearson Australia Group Pty. Ltd.)
Penguin Books India Pvt. Ltd., 11 Community Centre, Panchsheel Park, New Delhi—110 017, India
Penguin Group (NZ), 67 Apollo Drive, Rosedale, North Shore 0632, New Zealand
(a division of Pearson New Zealand Ltd.)
Penguin Books (South Africa) (Pty.) Ltd., 24 Sturdee Avenue, Rosebank, Johannesburg 2196,
South Africa

Penguin Books Ltd., Registered Offices: 80 Strand, London WC2R 0RL, England

This book is an original publication of The Berkley Publishing Group.

PRINTING HISTORY
Berkley JAM trade paperback edition / April 2008

Library of Congress Cataloging-in-Publication Data

Hale, Stephanie.
    Twisted sisters / Stephanie Hale.—Berkley Jam trade pbk. ed.
        p.   cm.
Summary: Fashion-conscious college freshman Aspen pledges a sorority in order to investigate the disappearance of Harry's niece Mitzi from Zeta house, and meanwhile, as her boyfriend, Rand, is kept busy by his new fraternity, his roommate Koop becomes obsessed with Aspen.
    ISBN 978-0-425-21950-8 (pbk.)
    [1. Greek letter societies—Fiction.   2. Universities and colleges—Fiction.   3. Missing persons—Fiction.   4. Dating (Social customs)—Fiction.   5. Mystery and detective stories.]   I. Title

PZ7.H138244Twi 2008
[Fic]—dc22   2007039878

PRINTED IN THE UNITED STATES OF AMERICA

10   9   8   7   6   5   4   3   2   1

For the chick I'd pick for my twisted sister any day, Lori Movick. Love ya, kitty!

Acknowledgments

Much love to my agent, and friend, Jenny Bent, for believing in my work and being honest when it kind of sucks.

Thanks to my editor, Cindy Hwang, and her assistant, Leis Pederson, for always making my books the best they can be.

To the Buzz Girls: Tera Lynn Childs, Tina Ferraro, Simone Elkeles, Heather Davis, Marley Gibson, and Dona Sarkar Mishra. The idea of a group blog has blossomed into so much more and I am honored to call each of you my friends. Check us out at www.booksboysbuzz.com.

To my book club, Chix n Lil, thank you for giving me something to look forward to every month. You have all been so supportive and have made me feel so special. I'm so lucky to be a chick.

To my family and friends who spread the word about my book, stalk teens in bookstores suggesting my book, and the ones who even read my book: thanks. I love you all.

To my three fellas, Warren, Carson, and Boston. Everything I do is for the three of you. I love you with everything I am.

And to all the people who buy my books! Thank you for allowing me to continue doing what I love. Thank you for all of the glowing e-mails and MySpace comments that you have all taken the time to write me. I read and respond to every single one so keep them coming!

One

"Don't be going all empty nest on me," I tell Mom, plopping my Juicy Couture–covered tush down on my overstuffed suitcase. I barely get the snaps locked without breaking a nail. Who knew leaving for college would be so much work?

"Can't a mother tell her daughter that she's going to miss her when she leaves for college?" Mom says, with a dramatic eye roll.

I turn to face her and strike my signature, hands-on-the-hips-you-better-pay-attention-to-me pose. "I'm going to miss you too, but I'm only an hour away. You need to get a hobby. I don't want you falling off the wagon while I'm gone."

"How dare you! I'll have you know that I've been

straight for ten months, three days, and eighteen hours," Mom shouts in fake outrage.

"Okay, okay. Chill out." Mom isn't a former crackhead or anything foul like that. She's a shopaholic, excuse me, a former shopaholic. I didn't even know there was such a disease until I found out last fall that Mom had pretty much wiped out any chance of me going to college by putting us in debt to the plastic gods. Here's the ad Master-Card doesn't run.

Mom with a shopping addiction
Several hundred shots of retail therapy: $8,000
Mail-order chasers: $3,000
Addict's daughter being forced to attend Comfort
    Community College instead of State University:
    Not so freaking priceless.

Luckily I found her a support group and returned most of the swag so we aren't totally busted in the funds department. I still worry though. I mean, I caught her red-handed trying to order by phone behind my back. I can only imagine how bad it would have been if my parents cared at all about keeping up with technology and had access to the Net. A shiver runs up my spine causing me to visibly shake.

"Aspen, I'm fine. I've dealt with all those old issues that caused me to overspend. I'm not going to tell you that I won't drool over the season's first pair of leather boots.

I'm a woman; it's genetically encoded in our DNA to love to shop. I've got my sponsor to help me if I start feeling vulnerable again," she says, wrapping her arms around me. I lay my head on her shoulder and inhale deeply. I'm going to miss that smell. The smell of home.

"I want you to go and have a good time. Don't worry about Daddy and me. You've had a tough year so the only thing I want you worrying about is having fun. Oh, and getting good grades," Mom continues.

As if Harry would let me forget that he expects a near-perfect GPA. Yeah, no pressure there. Detective Harry Malone and the Comfort Police Department are financing my college career. Not because I won some prestigious award or scholarship, but because I basically saved his career and he owes me. Not that he'd ever admit that!

Last fall, when I was a senior at Comfort High, really strange things started happening. At first they were just annoyingly outrageous, like a totally false statement about me scrawled in cheap lipstick on the girls' bathroom mirror at school. Then it started getting downright creepy; my tire got slashed, then my asthma inhaler got stolen nearly causing my untimely demise. As if me sporting a one-size-fits-all cotton-poly-blend hospital gown wasn't bad enough, then people actually started disappearing. I tighten my grip on Mom's shoulders as I remember the horrible, empty feeling I had when I found out Mom was one of the missing.

In retrospect, I think Harry really was doing everything

he could to find the kidnapper, but at the time I didn't think so. So I tied on my Nancy Drew cape and started my own investigation. In the end, I wound up hogtied next to Mom staring into the crazy eyes of my high school principal, Lulu Hott.

"I'm going to miss you too," I tell Mom once again, remembering how helpless I felt in Lulu's basement.

Mom pulls back, looks in my stunning violet eyes (what? They are), and knows exactly what I'm thinking.

"Lighten up, kid. This is going to be the time of your life. But just remember, sometimes people change and outgrow each other. It's just a fact of life," she says mysteriously before grabbing the heaviest suitcase and starting down the stairs.

I force a fake bubblegum-flavored lip-gloss smile and follow her down the stairs with my remaining suitcases. What was that all about? I'm not going to change. I'm going to stay the same fabulous girl I always have been. Parents are so out of it sometimes!

She is right about it being the time of my life though. I mean, Lulu is safely locked up in the sanitarium. Not that I'm afraid of her; we're actually kind of tight. We have an arrangement. I keep her stocked in monthly fashion mags and she gives me killer updos (even with handcuffs on) when needed. She wasn't really evil, just a little miffed about her tiara getting disrespected. Her original plan was to kidnap me just long enough to make me miss homecoming. She knew I'd be crowned queen (which I would have been if my HS nemesis, Angel Ives, hadn't totally rigged the votes, the beyotch!) and she wanted me to suffer the way my parents had made her suffer. She, kind of, used to date Dad, and he, kind of, sort of, dumped her for Mom. On homecoming. When it was too late to get another date. I know, the man is not a breakup etiquette genius. Lulu's brilliant plan got screwed up and she kept kidnapping the wrong people. She was getting desperate when Harry busted in and convinced her she wasn't unlovable. It turns out that *he* was in love with *her* in high school! Now that I think about it, it was all kind of six degrees of Lulu.

Except for the taser shock, the explosive diarrhea from the tainted chocolates that I gave her, and the seven years imprisonment in the sanitarium, Lulu's doing pretty good. She's even got her own line of Dooney & Bourke–toting Barbies coming out soon.

My parents are closer than ever since the kidnapping. Mom doesn't have to hide her addiction anymore. She's dealing with the core issues that caused the addiction. That's my fancy way of saying that she used to be a geek in high school, which totally caused residual issues. People just don't get how big of a deal your social standing in high school is. It totally carries with you for life. Thank God, I was an A-lister!

My life is nearly perfect again. I mean, I am still Aspen Brooks, which is pretty huge in these parts. The kidnapping made me an even bigger celebrity than I already was, if that's possible.

Mom swings open the front door and the very best part of my life is standing in the doorway. Rand Bachrach. Former geek turned chic and all mine. We've been exclusive for almost a year, but he's been crushing on me since pre-K.

"Hello, son-in-law," Mom greets him. She thinks it's funny to call him this. I so don't. I mean I know we are meant for each other, but to promote teenage marriage is just so wrong. I've considered calling her bluff and staging a fake justice of the peace wedding just to see her reaction, but I figure it would totally backfire on me. My parents love Rand so much that I've often wondered if I would be thrown out of the family if we ever broke up. I know they'd blame it on me. Rand can do no wrong around here.

Rand's eyes meet mine and I feel the familiar tug in my tummy that started when I realized I totally heart Rand. I adore that feeling. He moves swiftly around Mom, puts his enormous hands on both sides of my neck, leans in, and kisses me like it's the first time we've ever kissed. I drop my suitcases and wrap my arms around his neck, fully enjoying the kiss.

"Uh, excuse me. Parents present. Please put approximately twelve inches between your body parts," Dad yells, only half-jokingly, from the driveway.

I slide out of Rand's arms so Dad doesn't have a stroke. He still has a hard time imagining his little princess macking on some guy, even if it is Rand. It is going to be so stellar not worrying about curtailing excessive PDAs when we get to college. One of Rand's eyebrows darts up mischievously as he thinks the same thought. I was overjoyed when he turned down Harvard to follow me to State. State's not even close to an Ivy League school, but Rand's already loaded so it doesn't really matter where his degree is from. He already knows that when he graduates he'll take over his family's world-famous chocolate company. Someday I'll be the first lady of chocolate!

"Hey, boo," he says, finally, grabbing my suitcases and heading toward the door. I giggle as I follow behind him. Mom was right. This is the time of my life and I'm not going to let anything or anyone stop me from having fun. As if somehow psychically channeling my happy, carefree vibe and wanting to stomp it into the ground, Harry rolls up in his monster truck.

"Let me help you, Rand," Harry says, jumping out of his truck, taking a suitcase, and strategically placing it into Rand's dinky trunk. "The sooner I get her out of my town, the better." He laughs.

I counter by sticking my tongue out as far as it will go. "I see you've been slacking on your visits to the waxer," I point out, taking in his unibrow, which resembles an evil willy-worm.

"I'm not doing that anymore. It hurts too bad," he says, absently rubbing his face insect.

"You take good care of this young lady, Rand. Here, I brought this for you." Harry hands me a small pink gift bag. I can't help but giggle as his hairy arm holds the delicate bag out to me.

"Ooh, gifts," I shriek, yanking it out of his hand. My excitement quickly dies when I pull out a small silver whistle on a purple cord, a jumbo-sized container of pepper spray, a flashlight key chain, and the Spyderco Harpy knife that he had confiscated from the Lulu crime scene almost a year ago.

"Gee, you shouldn't have. Really," I say, not bothering to hide my disappointment.

"College campuses are one of the most dangerous places for young girls. Every three minutes a girl gets attacked," Harry says seriously. I watch the color drain from my parents' faces as Harry's statistic sinks in.

"Will you ever stop being such a buzz kill?" I ask, forcing myself not to kick him. The last thing I need is to have my parents freak and make me stay home and go to community college. They have been sort of overprotective since the whole Lulu incident. I'd probably end up working at Comfort Cozee Dogs, and let me tell you, a hair net would not be a good look for me.

"I care about you, Aspen, and I'm not going to apologize for trying to keep you safe. Just do me a favor and carry this stuff with you all the time," he says, making me feel totally guilty. I can't deny that we formed a bond over the Lulu incident. The least I can do is carry his poor excuse for a going-away present. I glance down at my teeny

Dooney & Bourke purse hanging off my arm and realize that the pepper-spray bottle won't even fit in there.

"I'll buy you a bigger Dooney, Aspen," Rand says, reading my mind. I jump up and down in excitement. I've gotten over a lot of my material attachments since last year, but Dooneys still get me every time. I don't miss the eye roll the guys give each other. Men just don't understand good purses.

"None of you have to worry, she'll be with me. And believe me, I know how to take good care of her," Rand says smoothly as he drapes his arm over my shoulders and gives me a little squeeze. Harry starts laughing, which he tries to cover with a fake cough. I, of course, am mortified.

Mom and Dad look on in horror as they wonder which is worse, a girl getting attacked on campus every three minutes or giving an eighteen-year-old boy brimming with testosterone access to his girlfriend twenty-four/seven.

"Okay, let's get going," I say, not wanting to give them any more time to debate it.

"Aspen, I was wondering if I could talk to you alone for a minute?" Harry asks, serious again.

Mom, Dad, and Rand look at each other puzzled. After everything we've all been through Harry should be able to say anything in front of Rand and my parents. Weird.

"Sure," I respond.

"It's just about the scholarship stuff, you guys. The

department insists on keeping some of the stuff confidential," Harry adds. My parents and Rand smile and nod, totally buying Harry's lame excuse to get me alone. What a bunch of amateurs! The detective obviously has something up his sleeve and it isn't just excessive arm hair.

Harry leads me to his manly overaccessorized truck. Even with the step boards, I can barely climb into the ten-foot high cab. How the man landed a hottie is still beyond me.

"Sorry about that, but I really wanted you alone for a minute," Harry begins.

I swear if he tells me the department is pulling my scholarship due to a lack of funds, my head is going to explode. I am so not staying home!

"It's about my niece. She disappeared off the campus last spring," he says, struggling to get the words out.

I feel the breath being sucked sharply out of my body. "Harry, that's horrible. I'm so sorry!"

I vaguely remember seeing missing posters of a pretty blonde around campus when I went for a visit a few months ago. I never gave her much thought, which makes me feel horribly guilty now that I know how upset Harry is. I had never even considered that people, like Harry, were going crazy wondering where she was.

"I didn't want to say anything in front of your parents and risk messing things up for you." He turns his head as a tear escapes his left eye.

I'm grateful, knowing if my parents caught wind of a

girl's disappearance, it would be community college all the way. I so could not handle that.

"She probably just got stressed out from finals and took off. She'll be back," I offer weakly.

"Her bed was covered in so much blood that she never could have survived. They just haven't recovered her body yet," he whispers.

"Oh, sorry," I say, hating that I can't help him like he's helped me over the last ten months. He's hairy and a buzz kill, but he's also a friend and I'd do anything to help out a friend.

"Listen, I'm sorry. I'm not trying to freak you out before you leave or anything. I just wanted to know if you are planning to join a sorority?" he asks, surprising me. Who would have thought that Harry would be interested in Greek life?

I perk up at the mention of rush, which I've anticipated since getting my acceptance letter to State.

"Does the Greek alphabet have twenty-four letters?" I answer excitedly.

"Um, I have no idea. Is that a yes?"

"Yes, it's a yes," I tease him.

"I know you well enough to know that I can't demand you to do anything," he says, gripping his steering wheel, "but I'm asking you, as a friend, if you could possibly not join the Zeta house," he finishes, dropping a bomb on me.

"Wh . . . Wh . . . Why?" I finally spit out, beyond stunned at his outrageous request. State only has four sororities and the Zetas have an excellent reputation for choosing only the finest girls. I really see myself as a Zeta girl.

"Mitzi, my niece, was a Zeta, and I can't help but think that more goes on in that house than keggers."

"You think someone in the house killed her?" I ask, incredulously.

"No, of course not. It's just that they are taking the whole sisterhood bond very seriously and aren't volunteering any information about Mitzi's life in the house."

I knew better than to get into a big debate about the importance of a girl's friends keeping her secrets. I knew he wouldn't get it. Guys never understand the depths of female friendships. I thought it was kind of noble the sisters weren't spilling all of Mitzi's skeletons the minute she disappeared. They were obviously of the motto, "What happens at the Zeta house, stays at the Zeta house," which I think is kind of cool.

"Does that mean you won't join the Zetas?" Harry asks, taking my silence as affirmation.

"Oh, hey, wait. I mean, what if I did rush Zeta, then I could get you some insider information?" I say, doing some quick thinking that would give me the best of both worlds. I'm always looking out for myself like that.

"Absolutely not!" Harry shouts, causing Rand and my parents to turn and look at us. I smile back at them and they go back to trying to defy the laws of space to find a place in Rand's car for all my luggage. They finally just give up and strap it to the top of the car. "You are not putting yourself in harm's way again," Harry continues, now in a full-on rant.

I hate to rub it in about how I pretty much solved his biggest case, single-handedly, only months ago, but I am about to anyway when Rand walks up to Harry's window.

"Ready to go?" Rand asks, looking gorgeous covered with sweat. I am so ready to go.

"Keep an eye on this one," Harry tells Rand, his cheeks reddening from the blood pressure spike I gave him.

"Are we clear?" Harry asks me, as I climb down from his truck.

"Crystal," I answer back, knowing that I am not eliminating myself from Zeta rush just yet. I mean, I'm already going to be rushing, how hard can a little recon on my soon-to-be sisters be anyway? Harry will totally thank me later.

"Oh, and Aspen?" Harry calls out as I walk toward my parents.

"Yeah?" I yell back over my shoulder.

"Just remember that there aren't any strings I'm above pulling to keep you safe." He laughs. He leans out his window and whispers something to Rand. Rand nearly topples off the step board he's laughing so hard. Guys. Sigh. Sometimes I just don't get them.

"What was that little exchange with Harry all about?" I ask Rand a few minutes later. I wipe the last of my tears from saying good-bye to my parents on his handkerchief. I think Rand is the last person under fifty who carries one, but it's one of the million reasons why I adore him.

"Just guy stuff," he answers cryptically, trying not to snicker.

"That's not fair. I tell you everything," I plead.

"Okay, then tell me why he had you over there in the first place," he tests me.

"He's freaked because his niece is the girl who disappeared off campus last spring," I tell him, knowing he'll remember the posters too.

"Oh, man. No wonder he was so hardcore about you being safe. That's horrible," he says, navigating his car through Comfort.

"He doesn't want me rushing the Zetas because he thinks they might be covering something up," I say, taking in the familiar sights of our hometown for the last time. I know that we probably won't be home until Thanksgiving and I want to remember everything. It's kind of a weird feeling, part of me wants to leave so bad, but the other part knows I'm going to miss everything here too.

"Harry's always had pretty good instincts; maybe you should consider his advice," he says calmly.

I can tell by the way Rand is gripping his steering wheel, a la Harry, that he wants to demand that I stay away from the Zetas, but he knows that would only result in me doing it out of spite.

"I'm going to think about it. Maybe I'll go through rush and not even like the Zeta house," I add, knowing that would take nothing less than a miracle.

"Yeah, maybe they're all a bunch of snotty, Coach-toting skanks," he says, doing his best imitation of me.

"You're hilarious. So how about spilling what you and Harry were gossiping about like a couple of school girls?" I say, putting my hand on his knee for a little extra persuasion.

"Look, we're here," he says, pulling to a stop in front of the house of our last good-bye.

I quickly forget all about the guys' secret as I remember how bad this last good-bye is going to sting. I get out of Rand's car and slowly make my way up to Tobi's front door.

"You look horrible," I tell Tobi, reaching up to touch her cheek. "Are you using that moisturizer I made you buy?"

"Yes, Aspen," she says, bristling at my touch.

"I'm going to miss you so much," I tell her, tearing up. Tobi and I have been inseparable since kindergarten and I still can't believe we won't be making college memories together. I know we'll always be bff no matter what, but I still know some days it will feel like I am missing an appendage without her there. Tobi had stood by me last year when I had basically accused her of teaming up with Angel and her cronies to destroy me. I felt like such a crap friend when I found out the truth. Tobi had been teaming up with one of Angel's cronies, Pippi, just not in the way I thought. Once we got it all cleared up that they were just lovers, I vowed that I would start being the best friend that Tobi deserves. I've done a bang up job so far.

"You're gonna set that place on fire, Aspen Brooks," Tobi says, sounding tired. "Besides, Rand will be there with you."

"Yeah, but I can't talk to him about makeup, clothes, and other boys," I say.

"Hey!" Rand laughs.

"You can't really talk to me about that stuff either," Tobi reminds me.

Tobi had been all set to start State this semester, then a few weeks ago, she called saying she had pulled her enrollment. She never gave me an explanation but I have a feeling it has something to do with money. I wish that I could pay her tuition myself. I'd give up all the Dooneys in the world to have Tobi on campus as my sidekick.

"Isn't there any way you can come?" I beg.

"Maybe next semester." She brightens, but I've known her long enough to know she's faking.

"It won't take you long to find a replacement for me," she says, grinning over at Rand.

"That's a horrible thing to say," I shout in outrage.

"Give me a hug and I'll beat it so you can do your girl

thing," Rand says, scooping Tobi into a hug. He tucks her stringy hair behind her ear and whispers something into it. She pulls away from him and doubles over with laughter. Rand chuckles and heads back to the car.

"I'd just love to know what everybody thinks is so hilarious," I say, tears rolling down my face.

"Oh, you'll find out soon enough," Tobi jokes, hugging me tight.

Two

As soon as Rand starts navigating his eco-car down Greek Row, I forget all about the whispering he refuses to spill about. Huge French Tudors and American Colonials with white pillars leading toward the sky sit side by side separated only by golf-course-manicured lawns. The houses are proudly accessorized with huge black wrought iron Greek letters. Most freshmen wouldn't have a clue how to tell a Zeta from a Delta, but I had already memorized the Greek alphabet at the beginning of the summer. I wasn't about to step on campus looking like an amateur.

"Not too shabby, huh?" Rand asks, braking to let some semidecent-looking guys wearing baseballs hats with Nu insignias cross the road.

"Won't it be awesome when we both live on Greek

Row?" I say, noting that the Zeta house shares a backyard with the Nu house. It couldn't be more perfect.

"Aspen, don't get ahead of yourself. We aren't even pledges yet," Rand says, following the oak-tree-lined road past the other sorority and fraternity houses.

"But soon we will be and it's going to be stellar," I say dreamily, allowing myself to remember how great the night that Rand and I were crowned prom king and queen was. I imagine our college years being exactly like that night only lasting for four years. Rand and I getting our pledge pins, being initiated in super-secret ceremonies, looking fabulous attending formals, and especially our senior year, when Rand will pin me. College is going to be four years of incredible memories with a few pesky tests in between. I can hardly wait to get started.

"We're here. Well, kind of," Rand says, interrupting my daydream of the next four fun-filled years. He pulls his car behind a line of at least one hundred other cars all waiting to enter the Towers. At first I think he's kidding because all I see is concrete, then I glance up and see my new home. Ugh! These are so not the digs I was imagining.

Our dorm is the largest in the world. It's like ninety-one meters tall; I have no clue how many feet that is; measurements have never been my strong point. The brochure says that when the wind blows you can feel the building move. I can't believe they actually think that is a good thing. Rand and I chose the Towers because it is the only coed building. As horrifying as it is to think of living in the same building with over one thousand college guys, it is even more horrifying to think of living all the way across campus from Rand.

Excited students crowd the sidewalk next to Rand's car hauling minifridges and futons into the lobby to begin the real task of making their way up to their floors. I'm a mix of nervousness and excitement about living away from home for the first time. The nervousness is mostly at the prospect of living with a complete stranger. I just hope she's as cool as I am. But what if she's not? What if she's a GDI? That's Greek talk for God damn independent, or someone who thinks they are too cool for the Greek way of life. I'm so down with Greek slang it isn't even funny. That would be *so* awful though! But I'm not going to stress myself out about it or I might get a zit or something foul like that.

Forty-five minutes and a few pounds lighter later, thanks to Rand's choice of no A/C due to the pollutants in Freon, he squeezes into a miniscule parking space in front of the Towers. It is the one, and I'm sure only, time I am thankful for his choice in automobiles.

"How many bags can you carry at once?" Rand asks immediately upon my getting out of the car. Jeez, so much for stretching and taking in one's new surroundings.

"What do you mean?" I ask him, puzzled.

He gives me this weird look as he unties the ropes against my luggage on the top of his car. One of my purple suitcases slams to the concrete.

"Rand, be careful," I shriek, running to assess any damage. At the last second before I unsnap the bag to check for wardrobe casualties, I remember the daunting task of getting it snapped in the first place and decide to put off opening it until I get to my room.

"Somebody takes these up for us, right?" I ask, leaning against the car.

Rand laughs loudly attracting a few stares from three blondes passing by. My eyes immediately lock in on the huge Zs on their tank tops. My stomach flips in nervousness at my first encounter with real live Zeta girls. I smile and wave. The girls don't give me a second glance, too busy ogling Rand's butt that is now directly in their view as he bends down to pick up my suitcase. I feel the rumblings of jealousy build inside me. This is not exactly how I pictured my first Zeta encounter would go. The girls whisper amongst themselves then disappear behind the building. Rand is completely oblivious to the whole scene.

As I watch him stack the bags the jealousy dissipates. Who can blame them for staring? Rand's a hottie. His normally pale freckled skin is lightly tanned from our many strolls in the park this summer. His hair is growing out and the natural curl he was blessed with causes it to flip up on the ends. I watch his adorable forehead crinkle as he counts the bags then glances worriedly up at our monstrous dorm. If anything, it just verifies what good taste the Zetas have and how good a fit I'm going to be in their sorority.

"We're going to have to make at least four trips," Rand tells me. Could he possibly be serious? I've already stripped down to my tank top because it is like a million and one degrees out here. And this humidity? Oh my God, my hair is completely fried.

"Are you serious?" I ask, tightening my ponytail.

"Aspen, this is not the time to get all diva on me. You're the one who had to bring so much crap," he says, wiping sweat off his forehead with the back of his hand.

Just as I am about to suck it up and grab one of the bags, a masculine hand intercepts my arm and takes the bag.

"Hey, let us help you to your room with those," the owner of the hand says. I look up and see the group of Nus we passed on our way to the dorm.

"You guys don't have to do that," Rand says nervously, being all considerate, making me want to slap him since I'm tripling my BO factor the longer I stand out in this heat.

"Let them help us, Rand. Do you really want to make four trips?" I ask, raising my eyebrow in a threat. Rand shrugs then hands a bag to one of the other Nus.

"I'm Brandon. This is Newt," the semihot hand owner says, pointing toward a big guy, "and Rich."

Rand extends his hand but doesn't introduce himself. It's kind of cute how nervous he is around these frat guys. I know secretly he wants in a fraternity as bad as I want in the Zetas. I think it would be validation for him that he isn't that geek from Comfort High anymore.

"You're Rand Bachrach, right?" Brandon asks finally when Rand doesn't offer his name.

"Yeah," Rand answers back shocked.

"I went to Comfort High. You were just a freshman when I was a senior. Good work sweeping the crown both times last year," Brandon says, talking about homecoming and prom.

Rand blushes, looking irresistible. I swear, I have the cutest boyfriend in the whole world.

"What are you doing here, man? I had you pegged for an Ivy Leaguer," Brandon continues, whacking Rand on the back.

"State has everything I need," Rand answers, squeezing my shoulder. Now it's my turn to blush. Brandon smiles at me, nodding in understanding.

"This is my girlfriend, Aspen Brooks," Rand tells the Nus, and the pride on his face is unmistakable. After all these months, I still love it when he calls me his girlfriend.

I hold up my hand in a greeting to the Nus.

"This place is killer on move-in day. The floors are so jacked. The elevators don't even go to every floor. Did you guys know that?" Brandon asks, starting toward the dorm. The other Nus grab our remaining bags and follow him. Rand and I trail behind making googly eyes at each other.

"What do you mean?" I ask, curious. This whole elevator not stopping at every floor thing doesn't sound good at all.

"The elevator only stops at every fifth floor, then if you don't live on that floor, you've either gotta walk up or down the stairs to get to your floor. Don't sweat it, you'll get used to it," he says, and then disappears into a giant turnstile.

"I still don't get this elevator thing," I say, still worrying.

"It's not too bad unless you have to walk up four flights of stairs. That gets kind of old, huh, Rich?" Brandon asks, nodding to Rich.

"But wait, wouldn't it be easier to ride up to the next stop and just walk down a flight?" I ask.

Brandon, Newt, and Rich drop our bags and simultaneously slap their foreheads.

"Why didn't anybody else think of that?" Brandon asks, amazed. I stand beaming, knowing once again I've dazzled everyone with my stunning wit.

We follow and get spit out into a giant lobby filled to capacity with stinky, sweaty bodies. The Nus start to head back toward the turnstile. They have obviously changed their minds about taking us all the way up after seeing the madhouse in the lobby. I can't say that I blame them. All these sweaty bodies make me want to run back to Greek Row as fast as my Target flip-flops will take me.

"Hey Rand, we're having an informal mixer at the house tonight if you want to stop by," Brandon yells over his shoulder.

Rand plays it cool even though I can tell he's psyched.

"Yeah, that sounds good," he replies.

Once they are out of sight I bounce up and down excitedly.

"Too much sugar?" Rand laughs, taking in our new surroundings.

"You're going to be a Nu! You're going to be a Nu," I singsong obnoxiously.

"Play it cool, babe. Somebody might hear you." He grins. I laugh even though I can't help but be a teensy bit jealous at how easy it was for Rand to score an invite from the Nus. The Zetas didn't even glance my way. I have some serious networking to do.

An older woman with megathick glasses holding a clipboard rushes over to us. "Names, please," she asks, interrupting our conversation.

"Aspen Brooks and Rand Bachrach," I tell her, praying she's not my RA, considering she's older than my mom.

She checks our names off her list then points toward a table across the room before scurrying off to the next student.

"I guess that was the welcome wagon." I laugh. The corners of Rand's mouth lift in a tiny smirk as he struggles to get our bags to the table. I'm starting to wonder if maybe I brought too much stuff. Nah, a girl can never have too much stuff. Once we get to the table we have to sign some official-looking document stating that we won't drink, smoke, or bring potentially harmful chemicals, weapons, or people into the dorm. Um, okay, whatev! We both scribble our signatures while trying not to crack up.

When I look up, a flash blinds me, and before I even know what happened someone is handing me a laminated ID card. I'm informed that this will be my ID for the entire time I am a resident of the Towers and losing the ID is pretty much going to get me a date with a firing squad. You'd think we were bunking with Prince Harry or something. I look down at the worst picture I have ever taken. I nearly scream as I take in my sweat-smeared mascara and frizzy humidity-ruined hair. This is so not cool. Rand chuckles beside me because he knows I'm about to lose it.

I wouldn't hate putting this whole college scene on pause for about twelve hours. I just want to get our crap up to our rooms, take a shower, then go and have a relaxing dinner with Rand. But as I glance around me, I realize none of those things will be happening anytime soon.

The lobby of our dorm is flooded with parents, students, and RAs. Tiny mailboxes line the entire west wall of the lobby. A huge counter surrounded by bulletproof glass takes up the entire middle of the lobby. Why in the world would they need bulletproof glass? I don't think I want to know. I notice that everyone is headed in the same direction, up a flight of about twenty stairs to a bank of ten elevators. Ten elevators for 2,200 students? Are they freaking kidding me?

"I guess we better get started," Rand says, carrying two suitcases and kicking a third, thankfully his, or he'd be getting an earful. That still leaves me with one too many. I can't believe that they don't have concierge service in a place like this.

The wait for the elevator is even longer than the wait to park. When we finally pile into the elevator, along with several people who smell like sausage, I think for sure I'm going to blow cookies. Especially when some wiseass starts talking about how often the elevators breakdown. I close my eyes and try to block out his voice. I also try and block out what a horrendous fire hazard my new home is.

A few minutes later, Rand squeezes my hand and we tumble out of the elevator.

"What floor are you on?" he asks, struggling with the bags.

"Taft," I answer back, breathing heavily. We both see the large green sign that reads, "Taft up four floors," at the same time and groan. Why the hell couldn't it have been down? At least next time we'll know to go up to the next stop. Of course that won't help with the suitcases this time though!

Rand swings the door open and we enter the stairwell and begin our ascent to Taft. He's on Roosevelt, one floor below me. I'm no history buff, but I know enough to know that President Taft would not be happy about this hike to his namesake floor. Pictures in our high school history books prove the man was not an exercise buff. You'd think the university would do more research before naming their floors!

"I don't think we'll have to worry about the freshman fifteen if we have to walk these babies a couple times a day," Rand jokes.

"This sucks. I can't make it," I say, collapsing on the second step. Rand looks around and seems to consider something.

"Okay, let's just leave some of it here. Nobody's going to bother it. Then I'll come back for it later."

"Are you mental? Most girls would claw each other's eyes out for the clothes that are in these bags. We can't just leave them," I tell him.

"Then get your lazy ass up." He laughs and continues up the stairs.

"Jerk," I mutter, half-laughing. We finally make it to my floor and I slide my foul-looking ID into a card reader to unlock the heavy steel door. It opens onto a lounge filled with orange and brown seventies-looking couches and fake wood coffee tables. Um, hello, where exactly is all of our tuition money going? Okay, so I'm on scholarship, but still.

Rand drops my bags and collapses in a heap on a couch. I plop down next to him.

"Please tell me every day isn't going to be this hard," I say, burying my face into his chest.

"Well, if this isn't just the sweetest thing I've ever seen," a syrupy voice says, causing me to bolt upright. I'm face to face with a plain twentyish looking girl with huge brown eyes and matching hair down to her waist.

"Hey, sugar. I'm your RA, Charlene. That's C-H-A-R-L-E-N-E, not S-H-A-R-L-E-N-E," she points out with a thick Southern drawl.

"I'm Aspen Brooks," I say, extending my due-to-move-in not-so-perfectly manicured hand toward her way-worse-looking-hangnail-ridden one. She grips my hand tightly and pumps until I'm afraid my arm might fall off.

"I thought you might be. Y'all are really late. All the other girls are already moved in," she says, causing me to flinch as I realize my roommate totally got dibs on the best bed and side of the room. "Those elevators are a bitch, ain't they?" she asks, startling us with a cuss word from such a delicate mouth. We nod. "Just wait until you've been here about a week. Then you get people pissing and puking in them. You ain't never smelled anything so bad," she says with a laugh.

Rand gives me a smile, knowing I'm in good hands, and stands to leave. "Nice to meet you, Charlene," he says. "I'm Rand Bachrach and you're going to be seeing a lot of me this year." He winks, grabs his bag, and heads toward the door. "Aspen, I'll catch you later." He blows me a kiss then disappears behind the steel door. My stomach lurches for a second until I realize that he's only going to be one floor below me.

"That is one fine piece of ass you got yourself there, missy. You better guard that with your life around here." She laughs, then grabs two of my bags. Between her and the Zetas, I'm beginning to realize that.

She gives me the grand tour. We stop at all the open doors and she introduces me to all the girls. Everyone is really nice. She lets me check out the bathroom, which is beyond foul. Group showers? It's so obscene. Not to mention doing your business in a stall next to five other people. And not a single bathtub? Lulu's digs in the sanitarium are probably better than this!

Our last stop is my room. The door to room 1547 is closed and suddenly I'm very nervous. I've never lived with a total stranger before. What if she is some completely unhygienic, annoying, horrible person? Charlene senses my fear and rests her hand on my shoulder.

"Don't tell anyone I said this, but your roommate is the sweetest girl here," she says, and then walks away leaving me to make my own introduction. I put down my bags and go to knock. Then I realize that it's my room too, so that doesn't really make sense. I push lightly on the door and it starts to open.

I can see that my roommate has chosen the bed closer to the wall, which pleases me. I wanted to be close to the huge window so it would help me wake up early. I push the door open farther. The room is really dark. No, wait, it's just that everything is black. A black-and-white comforter is draped haphazardly across my roomie's twin bed looking like a giant sudoku puzzle. A tall black Chinese lantern lamp sits in the corner behind the bed. A giant poster of Fall Out Boy is taped to the wall. This can't be. I'd always pictured my dorm room decorated tastefully in pink with feather boa and sequin accents placed strategically around the room. I'd imagined my roommate and I giggling over secrets while painting each other's nails. I never imagined séances to call evil spirits, which is the only thing this room looks good for. I don't even have to meet the girl to know that we have absolutely nothing in common. Maybe Charlene led me to the wrong room. That has to be it. I check the room number again. To my horror, it's correct.

What is wrong with the housing people anyway? Don't they compare our MySpace pages for compatibility before just sticking random strangers together? It's outrageous. I try to calm down and deal with the situation rationally.

Then I see her. Bent over a minifridge stocking Red Bull. Her ebony hair is pulled into two pigtails and her head is bobbing along with whatever is playing on her iPod. She's wearing a black wife beater and ripped blue jeans. She bends over, further, causing her shirt to ride up. My breath catches in my throat. On her lower back, I see a tattoo of Cupid slinging arrows toward a black heart. A name I can't read is tattooed under the heart, and even though I can't see it from here, I still know what it says. The name reads: Angel. I'd recognize that coin slot anywhere. Angel Ives, my former high school nemesis, turned groupie/stalker after our joint takedown of Lulu Hott. I back slowly out of the room with every intention of running like mad toward the housing office to beg for another room when she spots me.

She rips out her ear buds and comes full speed toward me. I keep backing up until I trip on one of my suitcases. I fall back against one wall of the hallway banging my head. I open my mouth to scream, but no sound comes out. Angel bum rushes me and before I can save myself, I'm caught in between her arms and a cloud of Curious that makes me dizzy.

"You're finally here. Can you believe it? We're going to be roommates! What are the odds?" she shouts joyfully, hugging me harder.

Pretty damn good, I think, recalling the whispers between Harry, Rand, and Tobi. How can Harry think that rooming with Angel will keep me safe? Harry always thinks he knows what is best for me, but he never does. He is going to get an earful for this.

Even though Angel and I agreed to a truce on trying to destroy each other after the Lulu incident, we aren't friends. We are like Prada and Payless. It's like trying to sequester Barbie and one of the Bratz dolls together in Barbie's van for nine months and expect them not to claw each other's eyes out. It's a disaster waiting to happen. Angel is a cheap, boyfriend-stealing, tiara-jacking skank. I'm a brilliant, sophisticated, timeless beauty. Okay, maybe Angel isn't that bad, but I still don't see how we will ever get through an entire year without killing each other, I think to myself, hugging her back.

Three

After two grueling hours trying to persuade Angel to add a little color to her side of the room (her response, black is the result of all colors, which, although factually correct, still doesn't help our dorm room not look like a funeral home), one shower with pathetic water flow while wearing heavy duty flip-flops due to fear of all diseases fungal, and trying to find an electrical outlet that Angel wasn't using for a potpourri pot, minifridge, two alarm clocks, and her iMac, I was ready to head downstairs to Rand's room to chew him a new one for not giving me a heads-up on my roomie situation.

"Where are you going?" Angel demands, walking through our door in nothing but a towel on her head.

"Um, excuse me. I really don't care to see your girl parts," I say, turning my head away from her.

"Lighten up, Aspen." I hear her open her rickety closet door and when I'm sure she is decent, I turn back around and head toward the door.

"Not that it's any of your business, but I'm heading to Rand's room," I say with my hand on the doorknob. "I can't take being in this room any longer. I think I'm getting that seasonal affective disorder. When exactly did you cross over to the dark side anyway?" I ask, still annoyed with her lack of decorating taste.

"I'm in mourning," she says softly, sitting on her bed pulling her long T-shirt over her knees.

"Let me guess. Wet n Wild stopped making that eyeliner you buy by the case?" I smart off.

She glances up and sticks her tongue out at me. "Not that you care but I'm mourning my parents' divorce," she says.

I don't think I could feel like a bigger beyotch if I tried. Everybody in our hometown knows about Angel's parents' divorce. Twenty-something years of marital bliss down the drain over a suitcase full of porn collected from the Las Vegas Strip. The whole ordeal was megatragic even if half the porn ended up in my locker.

"I'm really sorry, Angel," I say, losing my attitude. I'm not sure I'd sink to wearing black all the time if my parents broke up, but it might seriously affect my ability to accessorize.

Angel shrugs her shoulders, clearly not wanting to elaborate.

"Aren't you going to the recruitment parties tonight?" Angel asks, hopping up with renewed energy, digging through her already organized closet. I'd hung up my dressy clothes so they didn't get wrinkled, but I was too exhausted to do any more tonight. I just wanted to get some dinner with Rand and come back to crash on my germ-infested mattress. At least I'd remembered my bottle of Febreze. I'd used practically the whole bottle before putting on my sheets. You just can't be too careful when it comes to communal furniture.

"I'm not interested in joining the military," I say, halfway out the door.

"Recruitment for sororities, airhead," Angel says, looking at me with big bug eyes.

"The rush parties are tonight?" I shout. How did I not know this? And more importantly, how did Angel?

"Recruitment parties, Aspen, duh." She turns back to her closet pulling a hideous leopard print wraparound dress off a satin-padded hanger.

"You're rushing?" I ask, incredulously.

"Nooooo. I'm a potential new member going through recruitment. You really need to get the lingo down if you are going to go Greek," she answers, shaking her head in disgust.

"Let me get this straight. You're talking about being in

a sorority, right? You want to be in a sorority?" I repeat, just to make sure Angel gets what I'm talking about.

"When are you going to see me as your equal?" Angel asks, surprising me.

It isn't that I think I'm better than she is, just different. Really different.

"That's not what I meant," I defend myself.

"Listen, I know you have never liked me and I get that. What I did with Lucas while you were dating him was horrible, but I didn't do it to spite you. It just happened." A single tear falls down her face and she quickly wipes it away. I realize that this is the first time I have ever seen Angel Ives vulnerable and I don't like it. Angel has always been a formidable opponent because I knew she could always take my shit, no matter how much I dished out. Now that I've seen her crack, I know I need to pull back and consider her feelings. I've tortured her enough for the BJ she gave Lucas while we were dating.

"You're right. I've never really given you a chance," I admit. She looks up with surprised eyes. "I really didn't mean anything by it though. I'm just shocked that being in a sorority would appeal to you."

"My mom's a Beta legacy. They're really cool." She smiles, slipping into a pair of black patent stilettos.

"It sounds like you're a shoo-in, Angel. Not that they wouldn't pick you anyway," I say, choosing my words carefully. I have to admit Angel isn't really that bad. It's actually kind of nice to be rooming with someone who knows my history.

"Thanks," she says, beaming. "Now go get your quickie and get back here, pronto." She laughs.

"Angel, as if!" I laugh, heading out the door to Rand's room.

I bounce down the twenty stairs to the heavy steel door outside Rand's floor. If I keep up all this stair action, I'm going to come home buffer than I left. Maybe I won't have to find the rec center after all. I try my ID, but the door doesn't budge. Crap. I knock lightly hoping someone will take pity on me. Nothing. I bang a little louder not in the mood to go back down and get my cell to call Rand on his. The door suddenly flies open.

"Yum. Delivery for me?" a spiky-brown-haired, evergreen-eyed piece of man candy asks. He proceeds giving me a visual cavity search before I can even answer. In less than five seconds, I know that this is the type of guy who should be born with a skull and crossbones tattoo on his forehead.

"You wish," I counter, brushing past him and heading for Rand's room.

"What? Not even a little kiss? I've got the perfect place for those juicy lips of yours. Both pair, actually," his silky voice suggests behind me. I keep moving through the lounge trying not to gag at his comment.

"Wait up, gorgeous," he says, following me. "I'm Samuel Wynkoop the third, you know, of Wynkoop Pharmaceuticals. My friends call me Koop though," he says proudly.

Holy shit, Wynkoop Pharmaceuticals? Everyone in the entire world knows who they are, especially men over fifty with ED. Wynkoop Pharmaceuticals took the world by storm a few years ago when they put Viagro, their knockoff, and in my opinion, more appropriately named, version of Viagra on the market. Thanks to WP, now even homeless men can afford to have a six-hour erection. I try, very hard, not to let it show that I know this guy has more money than God.

"See ya, Sam," I respond, picking up my pace to lose him. He stays right on my heels.

Could he be any more of a predator? This is the kind of guy that moms warn their daughters about. I really want to turn around and give him a piece of my mind, but I know his type, he'd only see it as foreplay. I shake off his gigolo vibe and continue walking down the hall to find my devoted, sensitive, all-around good guy boyfriend. I can almost feel Mr. Man Candy's gaze searing into my butt cheeks as I go.

"Your loss, you snotty bitch!" he yells, as I turn the corner. The outrage! The bitch part I can handle. But I am so not snotty. I socialize with people from all classes. What a jerk! Where does he get off thinking he can talk to me like that just because I turned him down? I'm just about to turn around and start a huge scene when I realize that it doesn't really matter what some guy I'll probably never see again thinks of me. There are 2,200 people in this dorm; it's not like I'm going to be running into him all the time. I'm probably going to be meeting lots of jerks at college and I have to learn not to let every single one of them get under my skin. With that settled, I continue toward Rand's room.

All the floors of the Tower are set up exactly the same. When you walk through the heavy steel door there is the same cheesy seventies lounge that greets you, then three hallways branch off, each housing seven dorm rooms a piece. In a stroke of total kismet, Rand's room is directly below mine. I don't know why that makes me so happy; it's not like we'll be sending each other Morse code messages with a broomstick every night or anything, I mean if we want to spend the night with each other, we can. But we've already agreed that our academics come first. Neither one of us plan to be coming home for Christmas break with anything below a 3.5 GPA. That means we'll have to keep the romantic trysts to a minimum. But it makes me feel better just knowing that every night when I go to sleep, he'll be right below me dreaming of me.

I knock lightly on Rand's door. He greets me looking flustered and out of breath. A huge smile spreads across his freckle-sprinkled face when he sees me. It's amazing what that smile can still do to my insides!

"Hey, boo," he says, whisking me inside and flinging me down on his twin bed. This quickly reminds me that good grades won't be the only reason we choose to sleep alone most nights. Two anorexics couldn't fit comfortably on these germ-infested mattresses let alone two normal-size people. I bet that's why Angel picked the side closest to the wall, so when Lucas comes to stay for the weekend he can sleep smushed up against the cinder-block wall. How weird is that going to be? Waking up to see Angel and Lucas spooning each other. I'm okay with them being together but the thought of actually seeing it gives me shivers.

Rand eases himself down on top of me and starts nibbling on my neck. On a normal day, this is all it would take to forget whatever crazy things were happening in my life, but not today.

"Oh, no you don't, mister. You're cut off for not telling me about Angel," I say, pushing him halfway off me.

"Oh man, I totally forgot," he says, dying laughing. "Sorry, I needed that," he apologizes once he finally stops laughing. "This day just couldn't get any worse."

He looks so pathetic for a second that I pull his lips to mine. I've never had a day so bad that one of our kisses couldn't fix it. Rand starts getting a little more into the kiss than I intended, considering I'm going to have to bolt in about five minutes. I'm about to push him off me when a bright light suddenly blinds me and I'm face to face with Mr. Man Candy with Rand's hand up my shirt. And to think that just a few minutes ago I thought I would never see him again. As if I could be so lucky.

"Holy shit, dude. You gotta put a sock on the door if you're banging some slut so I know not to just walk in," he says, bouncing onto the plaid Ralph Lauren–clad bed next to us.

In less than half a second, Rand jerks his hand out from under my shirt, jumps off the bed, and is in his face.

"That's my girlfriend you're talking about, *dude*. You better watch your mouth or we're going to have a big problem on our hands." A vein in Rand's neck that I never even knew was there before is bulging. I know I should feel bad that I'm the cause of Rand's first fight with his horrible roommate, but I can't help feel a little giddy. Rand's never had to defend my honor before. It's kind of cool.

"Chill out, man," his roommate replies, putting his palms against Rand's chest. "It's just something I say. I didn't mean it literally." He laughs.

Ugh! After his comment at the door, I know he just said it because I didn't go for him. He's the type of guy who sees women as objects to be collected and discarded once he's done playing with them. I was probably the first girl to reject him his whole life, then he walks in on me with Rand. The slut comment was just a defense mechanism. To think, a few minutes ago, I thought *I* had a bad roommate.

"Listen, Randy. I don't want to fight," he says, plumping his pillow and leaning back into it.

"It's *Rand*! I've already told you that five times. You're just being a dick," Rand shouts in an angry voice I don't recognize. This has not been a good day for him. I bet right about now he's wishing he had gone to Harvard after all. I better try to smooth this over for him.

I pull Rand back onto the bed with me and clasp one of his hands in mine.

"I'm Rand's girlfriend, Aspen Brooks, and since we are going to be seeing each other so much we should probably call a truce," I say, laying on my charm.

He smiles devilishly, leans up, and takes my free hand. I feel Rand's grip tighten around my hand and I give him a squeeze to let him know I've got this under control. Mr. Man Candy/Predator looks me deep in the eyes, and says, "I'm Koop, but you already knew that. I was pissed about not getting a single, but I think now I'm kind of glad." When he doesn't let go of my hand, I shake it out of his grasp. This guy is a piece of work. I bet he had to come to college because he had already slept with everyone in his home zip code. Lucky for me, I've never fallen for guys like this. I know exactly how to deal with him. Watch and learn.

"Koop, you're a very good-looking guy. I bet you have to fight hotties off with a stick wherever you go." Rand hangs his head not knowing where I'm going with this. "But there is one thing you need to know about me," I continue, meeting the green fire in Koop's eyes head on. "I'm madly in love with this guy," I say, tilting my head toward Rand, causing him to look up, the grin on his face impossible to miss. "I can promise you that nothing you could say or do would ever change that. So can we just cut through all the bullshit and try to get along?"

Koop rolls onto his side and props himself up on his elbow. The cuffs of his polo strain against tanned muscular biceps. With his I-just-walked-out-of-a-styling-product-ad hair, perfectly filled-out burgundy polo, and even more perfectly filled-out khakis, I feel for all the girls past and future who will become his prey. It takes a strong girl to resist a package like that. He smiles, flashing pearly whites with a price tag that probably rivals a year of tuition at State.

"Okay, okay, I get it. You guys are doing the monotony thing. I respect that," he says.

"It's monogamy," Rand corrects him.

Koop nods innocently like his switch of words was a mistake. But I know better. This isn't the sort of guy who makes mistakes. I get the feeling that every choice he makes is meticulously planned out.

"Well, if you ever get bored you know where to find me," Koop says to me, sex practically dripping off him. I'm fairly certain that Rand's head is going to explode when an annoying rap song about bitches and hos starts blaring. Koop holds up his index finger gesturing for us to wait while he flips his cell phone open.

"Let's get out of here," Rand demands, pulling me up off the bed and dragging me out the door. I hear Koop's voice say, "You crazy kids wear a condom now" before Rand slams the door.

Talk about the roommate from hell!

It took me twenty minutes, but I finally get Rand calmed down. He heads off to his Nu mixer while I come back upstairs to get ready for my first round of rush, er, recruitment parties.

I'm glad that I had already done my hair and makeup earlier. I hated that I wasn't going to have more time to primp, but on the other hand, it didn't give me time to get nervous either so that was good. I slip into a black chiffon tulip skirt and silk aqua blouse. I skip the hose since I still have most of my golden hue from summer and step into my black Steve Madden stub-toed pumps. I go low-key with jewelry, and just pop in the diamond studs that Rand gave me for our six-month anniversary.

"Wow! You look incredible," Angel says, bursting through our door wearing a leopard-print dress and the brightest red lipstick I've ever seen. I force myself to think of something positive to say as I take in her heavily lined black eyes. At least she's wearing a color other than black.

"Is that a new nose ring?" I ask, taking in the gold hoop hanging out of her left nostril.

"Is it too much?" she asks, self-consciously touching the hoop.

"No, you look great. Let's jet," I say, grabbing my purse and heading out the door. Angel stops to lock our door then leads the way down the stairs to the elevator banks. I trail her as she maneuvers perfectly in her four-inch heels. The longer I stare at her, the more I realize that she really is beautiful in an unconventional way.

The doors open to an already packed elevator. Angel quickly crowds her way on and people willingly make room. I've always secretly admired that about Angel. She isn't afraid to go after what she wants. I stand outside the elevator, as the doors are about to close.

"On or off, Brooks," Angel says, smirking at me.

I skitter on the elevator right as the doors slam shut. I know at that moment with my beauty and brains and Angel's boldness and charm, we're a force to be reckoned with.

Four

State isn't a big Greek school. There are only four sorori-ties and seven fraternities. I never realized that might be kind of a problem, until now, as I watch at least two hun-dred girls teeter toward the Student Center in heels. The odds of getting selected by a good sorority are statistically stacked against me. Luckily my amazing attributes over-ride the statistics.

"Wow, I didn't realize so many girls would be trying to get into just four sororities," I point out to Angel, pray-ing I still have some Band-Aids in my purse because I can already feel a blister forming on one of my little toes.

Angel takes in the girls around her for the first time and shrugs. "If we get it, we get in. If not, I guess it wasn't meant to be."

I do a double take, wondering if this is really the same girl who rigged the homecoming queen competition last year so she could beat me out of *my* tiara.

"What? I've mellowed since my parents got divorced," she says, leading the way.

I realize that Angel had to grow up faster because of her parents divorce. Tiaras and sororities probably take a backseat after you watch your parental unit disintegrate. It would bite to have your parents split up, and I feel bad for Angel and her little sister. I know that I am lucky to have two parents who are still madly in love with each other, even if they embarrass me with their PDAs sometimes.

"That must be really hard. I'm sorry," I tell her.

"I just hate that I'm not around to protect my little sister. My parents are being so selfish, making her choose between them and buying her stuff to compete for her attention. It's so juvenile. She's really confused right now."

I see the glitter of tears shining in Angel's eyes as we pass under a streetlight. I know if all that black makeup starts running, she'll be screwed, so I quickly change the subject.

"I'm freaking starving. Are they going to have food at these parties?" I ask as we file into the auditorium and take our seats.

"I kind of doubt it. I don't think sorority girls eat." Angel giggles.

"Then I'm so not getting picked," I say, already looking forward to ordering my first college pizza later.

A hush falls over the excited girls as a microphone

screeches from a podium onstage. A petite redhead in khaki shorts and a pink T-shirt with Greek letters spelling Rho Gamma, steps forward. Her shirt confuses me because I thought the only sororities on campus were; the Zetas, the Betas, the Deltas, and the Sigmas.

"Hi, girls. I'm Tina and I'll be one of your Rho Gammas. Rho Gammas are girls who step away from their sororities to help you through the recruitment process. Don't ask us what sorority we are in because we won't tell you." She laughs. Several more girls in matching outfits line up behind her.

"Our fall recruitment is pretty laid back. Tonight you'll visit all four houses and mingle with girls from all the sororities. The houses are hosting a progressive dinner. That means you'll get a drink, appetizer, main course, and dessert, it just may not be in that order."

Giggles rise up from the auditorium from girls who obviously think getting dessert first isn't a bad thing. I'm one of them. My stomach is rumbling so loudly that Angel is periodically throwing me dirty looks.

The Rho Gammas explain the mutual selection process, which will weed out seventy-five percent of the girls tonight. Because State has so few sororities, the potential new members only get to pick one sorority at the end of the night. If you pick a sorority and they pick you, you're a new member. If not, you're out, even if another sorority picked you. It's kind of a Greek Russian roulette. Basically you have one night to make one heck of an impression or else you are banished to the land of GDIs for-eva!

I fidget in my seat, ready to get started.

"Okay, we're going to count off into four groups," Tina says, starting at the bottom row of seats. Girls start calling out numbers one through four. Angel quickly gets up and moves down a few seats, forcing a timid-looking girl out of her seat. The girl moves down into Angel's old seat.

"What are you doing?" I mouth to her, and then realize it's my turn.

"Three," I shout, thankfully remembering the number of the girl beside me.

A few seconds later, Angel calls out, "Three," and I realize what she was doing. She wanted to make sure that we got into the same group of recruits, which is beyond cool. I give her a thumbs-up and rise to meet her with the rest of the threes. I resolve from this moment on to be the roommate that Angel deserves and to put the past behind us for good.

There are about fifty of us and as much as I hate to admit it, I find some of the other girls intimidating to me as they talk about being legacies. Angel already decided that she wasn't going to pull her legacy card, which I think is insane. What good is a little nepotism if you don't take advantage of it?

Our first visit is to the Delta house. We form a single-file line on the sidewalk in front of the house and the Rho

Gamma leading us knocks on the front door of the huge Colonial mansion. Angel gives my hand a squeeze, which helps calms the waves of nausea that are rolling through my empty stomach. I can't believe how nervous I am just to meet a bunch of girls.

"Welcome, potential new members!" a crowd of girls in white Marilyn Monroe dresses and blond wigs scream. One by one the Deltas take a recruit by the arm and lead her into the house.

"Hi, Aspen. I'm Tulip," an extremely tall Delta says, reading my name off the name tags we were given before leaving the Student Center. She weaves her arm through mine and escorts me inside the Delta house.

"Hi, Tulip," I say, trying to keep a straight face. Who would name their kid Tulip? As I practically have to run just to keep up with her slow stride, I wonder if her parents knew she was going to have these serious stems when she grew up? Suddenly her name seems very fitting.

"Come on in and make yourself at home," she says, leading me through the grand marble foyer with a giant crystal chandelier hanging from the ceiling. Everything in the house is white and immaculate, even the fireplace. Tulip leads me into the great room that holds several rows of velvet wingback chairs.

"Here you go, Aspen. This will give you a perfect view of the show. I'm going to get you some dessert. I'll be right back," she says, disappearing from the room after taking just two steps.

Within seconds, she is back handing me a crystal bowl of jelly beans.

"Jelly beans?" I ask, hoping that she's joking.

"Aren't they perfect? Delicious and fat free," she babbles excitedly.

"Yeah," I agree, trying to keep the disappointment out of my voice. I pop a yellow one into my mouth and pretend it's a piece of lemon meringue pie.

"So, what's your major?" Tulip asks, playing with a curl in her wig.

"Pre-law," I answer, digging through the bowl to find more yellow jelly beans.

"That's great. My dad's a lawyer. He helps murderers go free," she says, reapplying blood-red lipstick.

"I was kind of thinking about taking a different route," I say, shocked by her statement.

Luckily the music starts, and Tulip bounds up the stage with the other Marilyns. They proceed to sing, "Deltas are a girls' best friend," in their best Marilyn voices. It's pretty cute; especially when fans under the stage start blowing their dresses up and they hold them between their legs Marilyn-style.

After the show, there is more mingling. By the time our Rho Gamma collects us for the next party, my teeth hurt. I just can't figure out if it's from the jelly beans or the sugary-sweet Deltas.

"I was going to hurt myself if I had to be there one more minute," Angel whispers, walking up beside me.

"Oh my God, I know. And since when are jelly beans dessert? That's just wrong," I say, my stomach still in outrage.

We laugh all the way to the Sigma house. We go through the same single-file line thing again. I'm starting to feel like I'm back in elementary school.

The Sigma house is gorgeous, but has a very anal feel about it, like there isn't a thing out of place. They even used clear plastic to make a path on the carpet, and I spot several signs telling potential new members to "stay on the path."

Their skit is a *Jeopardy* game show where pretty much every answer is, "What is Sigma, Alex." It is the lamest attempt ever to build up a sorority and now I feel like *I* might hurt myself if I have to stay any longer. I am thrilled when our Rho Gamma ushers us out of the house before we can mingle or finish our beverage portion of the evening (ice water).

"So, what did you think, Aspen? Do you want to be a Sigma?" Angel asks me jokingly, on our way to the Beta house.

"What is, no freaking way, Alex," I answer and we both crack up. Our Rho Gamma turns and gives us a dirty look. We had been warned earlier, before leaving the Student Center, about not talking between houses but I think that is a lame rule. Nobody is going to tell me that I can't talk. They might as well tell me not to breathe.

"I can't wait for the Beta house," Angel says, clapping her hands together.

A few seconds later, the door to the Beta house flies open and dozens of girls dressed like Belle from *Beauty and the Beast* flood out, singing, "Be Our Guest."

An ebony-haired beauty twirls around me whisking me inside. It's almost magical. They seat us on several white leather couches and reenact the end of the movie when all the dishes, furniture, animals, and humans turn normal again. I can't help wondering if they are all drama majors from the high quality of their skit. It makes the other two skits look like they were produced by five year olds.

After the skit, my Belle and a few others, approach me with two pieces of garlic bread with cheese and a Coke.

"Oh my God. You guys are lifesavers," I say, scarfing down the food. I'm too famished to be self-conscious, but I can tell the Betas don't care anyway.

"Aspen, I love your Dooney," the Belle on the right side of me says, touching the purse hanging off my arm.

"Thanks, I'm kind of an addict," I say, between gooey bites.

That's all it takes for the three of us to start an in-depth conversation about the many faces of Dooney. After we've exhausted that topic, we discuss boys, where I brag on Rand endlessly, and the girls can't get over how cool it is that I can get free boxes of chocolate anytime I want. They clue me in on the best classes to take and the teachers to steer clear of. I'm genuinely disappointed when our Rho Gamma herds us out the door.

"Aren't they incredible?" Angel asks, obviously smitten.

"They really are," I say. I'm torn because I wasn't expecting to be so comfortable in another house. I had always seen myself as a Zeta girl, but I have to admit that the Betas hospitality and soft sell won me over.

"Okay, I know it's been a long night but this is your last house," our Rho Gamma says, knocking on the door of the Zeta house, "and we always save the best for last."

"Oh my God, she is so not supposed to show preference," Angel whispers in outrage. "I should turn her in to the Panhellenic council." She jams her fists on her hips and glares at the Rho Gamma.

"Chill out, Angel. I have heard pretty good things about the Zetas," I say, not remembering exactly where or who I got my information from. How exactly had I gotten it in my head that the Zetas were the best sorority on campus? I couldn't remember right now but I was sure they were about to prove me right.

The door flies open and girls in bikinis come running out. All the potential new members look around in confusion wondering if we missed the sign for the carwash. A brunette in a Burberry bikini runs up and grabs my arm dragging me in the house.

"Hi, Aspen. I'm Mary-Margaret," she says, extending her bronze arm through mine.

"Hi," I say, still stunned at the Zetas lack of attire. They all have killer bods, but it was like they knew that and wanted to show off. I let Mary-Margaret lead me into the Zeta house while trying to force myself to think positive.

As with the other houses, the Zetas put on a skit in the great room. The Zetas' sketch is a beauty pageant, similar to the Miss USA pageant that I watch faithfully every year, except that instead of the girls representing states, they are representing the four sororities on campus.

A Zeta dressed as Little Bo Peep wears a sash that reads, "Delta." A geeky girl with pop-bottle glasses has a Sigma sash across her white button-down oxford. And a girl dressed in a polo and khakis wears a Beta sash. I don't get that one until the preppy girl turns around to flash a sign that reads, "Scholarship Recipient." Oh, that is so not right. I'd be totally offended if I had gotten my scholarship because I was poor. Someone crowns the beauty in a gold evening gown, tiara, and Zeta sash the winner. The other Zetas jump up and down cheering for her. Okay, so I guess the Zetas skit is to bash on all the other sororities.

I'm not really in the mood to mingle so I slip out of the great room and up the stairs to find a bathroom. The wall up the stairs is lined with framed photographs. Most are collages of individual shots of each sorority member wearing a black dress and pearls. As I survey each member, I wonder what made me think that I was going to fit in with a bunch of snotty blue bloods.

Then I see Mitzi's picture and I feel nauseous. She is smiling brightly and doesn't look like she has a care in the world. *Where are you, Mitzi?* I wonder to myself. Could the smiling beauty in this picture really be dead? And if so, did one of these girls know who killed her? I don't even know why I care so much, I didn't know her, then Harry's face pops into my head and I get it.

Harry irritates me like a harsh exfoliant but I love him. He's like a really unkempt, annoying uncle. He saved me and my mom from a very untimely demise last year and I owe him. Here I am with the perfect opportunity to go deep undercover to find out what happened to his niece. I can't pass that up, can I?

"What's with the girl in the spots?" I hear a nasally female voice ask. I duck into a deep doorway to keep from being discovered upstairs.

"I know, like the zoo called and it wants its cheetah back," another girl responds, laughing.

I want to jump out into the hallway and pound them for talking shit about Angel. Nobody is allowed to do that except me. But if I'm going to be a Zeta pledge to try and find out what happened to Mitzi, the last thing I need is a confrontation. The girls laugh and finally pass by, not having a clue I'm there. I watch their barely covered-by-bikinis butts swagger back downstairs to the great room.

I bend down and dig a Band-Aid out of my purse. I slip my foot out of my pump and wrap the bandage around my little toe, which has a mondo blister on it. I lose my balance trying to stand on one foot and reach out to brace myself against the door I'm standing in front of it. Suddenly, as if in slow motion, the door flies open and I fall flat on my face on the carpet.

"Are you all right?" I hear a girl ask me.

"Yeah, I think so," I answer, struggling to recover from getting the wind knocked out of me. The girl helps me to my feet and I take in my surroundings. I've fallen into one of the sisters' bedrooms. I can't believe it. I actually penetrated the inner sanctum of the Zeta house by acting like a total dork.

Standing in front of me is the most beautiful girl I've ever seen. Not movie star pretty or runway model pretty, but like glossy-airbrushed-doesn't-really-exist-on-this-planet pretty. For a second, I wonder if she is a mirage. I want to reach out and touch the silky black hair that falls lightly against her shoulders. Her eyebrows are such perfect arches they look drawn on with a charcoal pencil. Thick spidery lashes hood twinkling emerald eyes. She's dressed in innocent Britney. A white button-down oxford with a gray cardigan layered over it. She's tall, at least six inches taller than me, and her tartan plaid skirt hits her perfectly in the muscular crease of her thighs. From the knees down, she is wearing navy knee socks and black Mary Janes. I was under the impression that the only time black and blue go together is to form an ugly bruise, like the ones I'm going to have after this fall, but this girl is stretching fashion boundaries and excelling. I can't stop staring at her. She's that pretty. I feel weird. Like maybe I don't look that good, or what if my outfit looks stupid, or what if I've got jelly beans stuck in my teeth. I think I feel self-conscious. Oh my God, how do normal people deal with this feeling of inadequacy all the time?

I still haven't said anything. What if I sound unsophisticated?

"I'm Charm," she says, extending a graceful hand that is probably insured by Lloyd's of London.

"I'm Aspen. Sorry about busting in. I was just putting a Band-Aid on a blister," I explain, trying to regain a tiny bit of composure.

"You must be going through rush." She nods, knowingly.

"Yeah, but I don't think we are supposed to call it that anymore," I say, immediately feeling like a know-it-all.

She slaps her hand over her mouth and her eyes bug out.

"Don't tell a soul I said that or I'll be banished forever." She laughs.

I instantly like her and can't believe she shares a house with the other stuck-up beyotchs downstairs.

"So where's your bikini?" I joke.

She rolls her eyes and says, "Well, I just couldn't decide which thong to wear so I decided to stay in and study instead."

"But classes haven't even started yet," I say, amazed that someone would actually study before they had to.

"I like to get a head start." She shrugs.

I glance around the spacious room at the pristine white canopy twin bed, matching vanity, desk, and giant armoire. Nice digs. Two piles of textbooks five deep sit next to the desk. Framed photos and a laptop sit on the organized desk. I can't help but notice the stark emptiness of the other side of the room. The furniture is all the same but there are no sheets or comforter on the bed and the desk lacks any personal effects.

"It's probably cool having a single," I say.

A strange look crosses her perfect features but she quickly recovers.

"I'll be able to get a lot of studying done," she says, turning her head away from me.

"I can't believe somebody isn't begging you to let them move in," I say, soaking in the room. I've only been bunking at the concrete jungle for a few hours and I'm already looking to trade up.

"My roommate disappeared last semester. I guess people think rooming with me would be creepy," she says, getting misty eyed.

I try so hard not to show the shock I'm feeling at her confession. I can't believe that this great girl is Mitzi's old roommate. It is too weird.

"What happened to her?" I probe delicately.

"I don't know. She just disappeared," she says, shaking her head. "One day I came home and her bed was filled with blood. Nobody ever saw her again. I'm so sorry. I'm not even supposed to be talking about this," she says, acting guilty.

"It's okay if you want to talk about it," I say, trying gently to pump her for information. I hate taking advantage of such a nice girl but then I remember that when you are working undercover, you just can't worry about people's feelings.

"I'm fine, but thanks. You better get back or they'll be sending the bikini squad after you," she says with a laugh, in a good mood again.

"It was nice to meet you, Charm," I say, heading for her door.

"I really hope I see you again, Aspen. Bikinis aside, the Zeta house really is a great place to be." She smiles then dives right back into her textbooks.

I show myself out and sneak back downstairs.

"There you are, Aspen," Mary-Margaret says, rushing toward me with a small platter. Another bikini-clad girl follows her and waves at me. It's not a normal wave though, as she is sucking her thumb and just waves her remaining four fingers. I had almost forgotten how incredibly hungry I was. The Zetas were in charge of the main course. My mouth watered imagining succulent prime rib or fresh lobster tail in drawn butter.

"This is Jocelyn. Want some sashimi?" Mary-Margaret

asks, thrusting a platter filled with tuna at me. Gag! Have these people not heard you can get worms from eating raw fish? And is that girl really sucking her thumb?

"I'm pretty full," I lie, looking away from the platter before I hurl.

"Okay, more for me," she says, popping a piece of tuna in her mouth. Between bites she babbles about how great the Zetas are and how she was nothing until she became a sister. Jocelyn never says a word or takes her thumb out of her mouth. I notice a group of girls in the far corner eyeing me like I'm a pair of Jimmy Choos on clearance. I smile at them and they scowl in return. I want to do nothing more than run screaming from this house but then I remember that I have the perfect opportunity to help Harry. And I really do like Charm. If she lives here, surely all the girls can't be that bad. They just need to get used to me then we'll be like long-lost sisters, pun intended.

Soon our Rho Gamma is rounding us up to head back to the Student Center.

Angel gallops up next to me with the same pep she started the evening with while the rest of us are seriously dragging ass.

"So, it's a no-brainer, huh?" she whispers.

I know in my heart I want to go with the fun-loving Betas, but my conscience won't let me do it. I have to at least try and get Harry some answers. Last year I was completely self-absorbed, but here I am this year, willing to sacrifice the most important social decision of my college career. I've matured so much in the last year it isn't even funny.

"Yeah, a no-brainer," I answer back, not meeting Angel's eyes, heading toward the Student Center to write down my sorority preference.

Five

Three days have gone by since I sealed my fate in a white envelope at the Student Center. I know that Angel was peeking as I wrote down my choice so I covered up the *Z* so she could only read *eta*. I know she assumes I chose the Betas and I feel guilty about it. And sort of depressed because I'd really had a good time with the Betas, but my loyalty to Harry won out. I know that Angel will be okay without me, but it doesn't make me any less scared for her to find out what I've done. She is busy organizing her desk, whistling away.

"Can you believe the obscene amount of money we had to pay for these textbooks? It almost makes me feel bad for my dad," Angel says, laughing sarcastically. Her cell phone rings cutting off our laughter. She takes it from her pocket, checks the display, and then slips it back into her pocket.

"Someone completely unworthy of your time?" I joke.

"Yeah, kind of. Lucas." She sighs. Her phone stops ringing and our dorm phone immediately starts ringing. I gesture toward the phone and she shakes her head no.

"What's up with that?" I ask her. Lucas and Angel had been joined at the hip since the kidnapping incident last year. Lucas had blown me away by showing actual depth in his feelings for Angel. All the time I was dating Lucas, I'd just thought he was a pretty face. Plus I had to give him snaps for lending a hand in the homecoming-vote scheme to try and get Rand and I together.

"I don't know. I just think that maybe it would be better if we went our separate ways since I'm here and he's still back in Comfort," she says, not meeting my eyes.

"Wow, I didn't see that coming," I admit. Lucas lets our phone ring at least ten times before hanging up. As annoyed as I am that our dorm phones don't have voice mail, I feel bad for Lucas and it gives me chills to think that Rand and I could have ended up the same way if he had gone to Harvard. Long-distance relationships just never work.

"I'm going to tell him," she mumbles when our phone starts ringing again, "soon."

"If you want to talk about it, I'm here," I offer, digging through my closet for something to wear tonight. It's finally preference night when I'll find out if the Zetas picked me or if I'll spend the next four years being a GDI. I hate that part of me thinks I would prefer the latter.

"Maybe some other time." Angel smiles over at me and I can't help but be stunned that we are actually bonding.

My cell phone vibrates in my pocket. I pull it out and check the screen. It's Rand, which makes me incredibly happy. Between recruiting/rushing/whatever we haven't gotten to see much of each other lately.

"Hey, you," I answer in a smoldering voice, which makes Angel giggle.

"Hey, boo," he says in a less than enthusiastic voice.

"What's wrong?" I ask, worried.

"Oh, nothing, besides the fact that soon there is going to be a bird flu pandemic and Wynkoop Pharmaceuticals is going to be the only company who can cure it."

"Huh?"

"That's what I get to listen to all day. I swear, if I hear about this magical cure one more time I'm going to march down to the dining hall and stick myself in the eyes with sporks." Rand laughs.

"Just look at it this way. Koop is such a shell of a person that all he has to brag about are his father's accomplishments. He's all frosting and no cake."

"Oh, God, please don't start with the dessert analogy again, Aspen. I'll quit bitching."

"Why don't you just come up here?" I plead.

"I'm not leaving so you guys can get it on," Angel yells in the background.

Rand laughs. "I can't. We are supposed to report to the house at four and they told us not to expect to be home all night," he says, trying to fight the excitement in his voice.

I know how important it is to him to fit in and I'm happy for him, even if it kind of blows that we aren't seeing each other a whole lot.

"That's cool. Tonight is our preference night so I'll be gone too," I remind him. Angel claps her hands with glee at the mention of it.

"Have you told her yet?" Rand asks, hearing Angel's clapping.

"Um, no," I reply secretly. I have no plans to clue Angel in about my scheme to infiltrate the Zetas to find out what happened to Mitzi. Part of me still can't believe I'm even doing it. I hope I'm not one of those adrenaline junkies who always has to do crazy things to be satisfied with her life.

"Aspen, you should at least warn her. I ran into her on the quad today and all she could talk about was being sisters with you."

Rand's words kick the guilt in full blast. But I'm not budging. I know that Angel will be so wrapped up in the excitement tonight that she will barely even notice when I don't get into the same sorority.

"Not gonna happen," I tell him.

"Fine, whatever, but don't come crying to me when this whole thing bites you right in the ass."

"You want to do what?" I tease him, shifting topics

before he has a chance to realize that I might be putting myself into danger by getting close to the Zetas. He is a typical male when it comes to sororities. His first thoughts are pillow fights and panty raids. Like every other male alive, he doesn't comprehend the evil that can lurk under the lip gloss and nail polish. And that's where I come in.

I'm sitting on a hard plastic chair in the lobby of the Student Center surrounded by nervous girls. We are all holding white envelopes that hold our futures in them. I keep twisting mine over and over trying to see through it with no luck. Do they give you an envelope even if you didn't get picked? Surely not, that would be seriously cruel.

I am glad that the Rho Gammas seated us when we walked in and placed Angel and I away from each other. This whole scene is going to be hard enough; I don't think I could stand to be right next to her when we rip the envelopes open.

"Okay, girls. Are you ready?" the Rho Gammas shout in unison. Screams erupt from all around me but not me personally. Even though I feel adorable in my plaid wool skort and cranberry-colored cashmere V-neck, I can't get into the spirit of the night. Something just feels off and I can't put my finger on it.

"Okay, rip," the Rho Gammas yell. The sound of envelopes tearing fills the air. I slide my manicured fingertip under the flap and tear mine open. I pull out the white note card inside and flip it open. In hot pink curly script is the word *Zeta*. I am officially a Zeta.

Screams and sobs fill the lobby as girls run to their new sisters. I spot an ecstatic Angel waiting for me in the first aisle. I try to return her smile but I know it is a pathetic attempt. I get off the seat, smooth my skort, and head toward her. From the corner of my eye, I note the Zetas huddling together watching me. I feel the pull of their eyes the closer I get to Angel.

She holds up her card that reads, "Beta," with the enthusiasm of a five-year-old with a new toy. I don't know how to tell her. I don't want to hurt her. I know now that Rand was right, I should have warned her, it wasn't right to do it this way. But it's too late. There is no other way. I hold up my card, shrug my shoulders, and turn toward my new sisters.

"Congratulations, Aspen. Welcome to the Zeta house," the house president, Cassandra, says. I remember her because she reminds me of a Bratz doll I used to have with her huge cat eyes and fat Botoxed lips. All the other sisters just stand and stare at me but don't say anything. It's sort of creepy.

"Here, put this on," Cassandra says, slipping a hideous purple sweatshirt on over my fabu sweater. The sweatshirt has a huge pink *Z* on the front of it.

"Oh, okay, thanks," I say, trying to be grateful, knowing that I'll rip it off the minute I'm out of their sight. The other sisters come alive as I slip into the sweatshirt and start hugging and congratulating me.

I glance over my shoulder to see Angel being swarmed by Betas. They are fussing over her like she is a queen, which she should love, but from the sad look on her face as she glances back at me, I can tell she doesn't even notice.

Slowly the groups file out of the Student Center to go back to their houses and celebrate. Angel gets swallowed up by the Beta crowd and taken out the door.

"Where are all the other recruits?" I ask, noticing how small our group is compared to the other sororities.

"Oh, you're it this semester. We didn't really want any new members this semester, but the council insisted we choose at least one girl. So you're it," Cassandra says, flipping her hair back. Gee, make a girl feel special why don't you? I've never been an obligatory choice before and I don't like it. I try to blow off her snippy comment and look around for Charm, knowing that seeing her will make me feel better but she's not here.

"Let's get this party started," one of the sisters says, leading the way out of the Student Center.

I smile, thinking maybe this won't be so bad after all. Maybe I will find out the sisters didn't have anything to do with Mitzi's disappearance and they will become my best friends. Not that I could ever replace Tobi, or Angel, even though she will probably never speak to me again.

"Oh, no, sweetie. Not you," Cassandra says, placing a hand on the Z in the middle of my sweatshirt. "This party is just for initiated sisters. You've got to earn the perks of being a Zeta," she smarts off. I take a step back, stunned by her sudden attitude, and her hand falls to her side. I'm not used to being manhandled even if she is a girl.

"Come to the house first thing tomorrow morning," she says, turning to go. All the other sisters give me a hug and a wave before disappearing out the door leaving me all alone in the Student Center.

I collapse into a chair trying to figure out if that really just happened. I glance around at all the discarded envelopes that the girls had held as delicately as flowers just a few minutes ago. I couldn't help but feel like one of those shredded envelopes. I wasn't expecting fireworks and a parade, but a pizza party would have been nice. Or just an invitation to my own damn party. I guess I am so used to being royalty at Comfort High that being a frog at State is going to take some getting used to. I don't like it, but I know I'll be back on top in no time.

I shake off the icky rejection vibes, fling my purse over my shoulder, and take off across the dark campus. I try not to glance down Greek Row but it is impossible not to miss the lights blazing and speakers pounding at every house. I can't help but be a teensy bit jealous of Rand and Angel, which I hate.

I try to think positive as I make my way back to the dorm. This will be good. I could use some me time. I'll run myself a frothy bubble bath and spend the evening pampering myself with exfoliates and lotions. Crap, no bathtub.

No problem, I'll just curl up and watch my favorite chick flick. Crap, no DVD player. Okay, so what could I do, I wonder, pulling my arms around myself to fight off the sudden cold snap.

Pizza. I could order a greasy pizza and watch reruns on Angel's TV. That could work. I'm busy figuring out which toppings to order when, from out of nowhere, a strong arm grabs my waist and pulls me off the sidewalk. Before I can even register what is happening, I'm pinned against a tree. I'm about to scream when a salty palm gets slapped over my mouth. I'm too pissed to be scared. I'm going to be one of Harry's freaking statistics. The arm spins me around and I get my first look at my attacker. Samuel "my friends call me Koop" Wynkoop III.

"I'm not going to hurt you, Aspen," he clarifies, immediately releasing me. "Why would Rand ever let you walk alone on campus at night? If I was your boyfriend, I'd never let you out of my sight," he says, bracing his arms above me on the tree and fixing his magnetic green eyes on me.

"That's not a boyfriend, that's a stalker, Koop. And I don't need any help taking care of myself." I'm all jittery from the adrenaline overload and the scare that he gave me.

"You need me, you just don't want to admit it," he says, leaning his face closer to mine.

I quickly weigh the use of excessive force and determine that it is justified for this particular situation. I lean in toward him, close enough to feel his breath on my face, while pulling my left arm back and making a fist with my hand. Just as he moves in to kiss me, I punch him in the middle of his chest as hard as I can. He stumbles back, dazed. I scurry toward him and raise my right leg as high as I can. I use every bit of gam power I've got to bring the heel of my boot crashing down into the side of his left foot. He screams an intelligible mix of obscenities right before I pop him in the nose with my left fist. His nose starts squirting blood right before I kick him square in the twig and giggle berries. He drops to the ground with a thud and puts his hands up as if to admit defeat. I knew watching all those reruns of *Miss Congeniality* would pay off. I am so proud of myself for remembering the character in the movie, Gracie Lou's, self-defense technique: solar plexus, instep, nose, and groin. I am so writing Sandra Bullock a fan letter!

I can't believe nobody else was around to see me totally kick Koop's ass. What a waste of adrenaline.

"Jesus, all right, you can take care of yourself," he says, out of breath.

"You bet your tight ass I can." Oops, did I say *tight* out loud?

He grins evilly and I know I did. I hate that Koop does get to me a little bit and decide to put an end to our alone time by making use of Harry's whistle to bring some attention to myself. I pull the tiny silver whistle out of my purse and place the cold metal to my still glossed lips. That Clinique lip gloss will last through anything!

"You're a Zeta?" he asks, distracting me.

"Don't try to distract me. If I blow this thing, everything in a ten-mile radius is going to hear it," I threaten, lowering the whistle.

"Go ahead. You're in way more danger with your new sisters than you will ever be with me," he says, defeated.

"What do you know about the Zetas?" I ask, hating that I'm curious about anything he would have to say.

"The Zetas are a messed-up bunch," he says, wiping blood from his nose on the grass next to him.

I dig a Kleenex out of my purse and hand it to him while dropping the whistle back in.

"How would you know anything about the Zetas?" I ask snottily, knowing he's full of crap.

"Everybody knows. Stuff gets around campus pretty quick," he says, offering no actual evidence to support his claim, just as I had expected.

"You are so full of shit your eyes are turning brown," I say, stomping away from him.

"Haven't you heard about Mitzi Malone?" he asks, stopping me in my tracks.

"What about her?" I turn and ask him, nearly dying of curiosity.

"She was a Zeta. One morning her roommate found her bed full of blood and nobody ever saw her again." He isn't telling me anything I don't know but it is still creepy to hear it in the pitch dark with a guy who could possibly be deranged.

"That could have been totally random. Just because she was in the Zeta house doesn't mean they did something to her. And what do you care anyway?" I demand, disgusted that I let him get to me.

"She was my girlfriend, that's why."

A half hour later we are sharing a pizza on the floor of Angel's and my dorm room. This is the last thing I expected to be doing tonight.

"I think maybe we got off on the wrong foot," I say to Koop, shoveling in a bite of greasy pizza.

"Not really. I was just an epic dick today," he replies, to which I nod in agreement. "It was hard seeing you guys together knowing that I wouldn't be with Mitzi," he admits, leaning back against Angel's bed.

Our dorm phone rings before I can comment on the fact that he was a dick way before he saw me with Rand. And if he was so heartbroken, why did he hit on me the minute he saw me? And make those comments tonight? I actually already know the answer to these questions. Koop is a typical man-whore. He is still in love with Mitzi but just can't stop himself from trying to attain the unattainable: me. I suppose I can't really blame him. I have that effect on men.

I know that being alone with him isn't the smartest move I've ever made, but as creepy as he can be, I just don't feel like he is actually dangerous. And I have to find out what he knows about Mitzi's disappearance. I grab the receiver off my desk and stretch it down to my ear.

"Angel?" Lucas's desperate voice asks.

"No, Lucas, it's Aspen. I live here too, remember?" I roll my eyes at Koop even though deep down it feels good to be talking to someone from home.

"Hey, Aspen. How are you?"

"Pretty good. Listen, Lucas, I'd love to chat, but Angel's not here and I have company. I'll leave her a message, okay?" I rush him off the phone, afraid that Koop might get spooked and leave before I can get any Mitzi info.

"Sure, tell Rand I said, 'hey,' " he adds.

"Oh, it's not Rand, but I'll tell him."

"You're alone in your room with another guy?" Lucas shouts.

"It's not like that, Lucas. Chill out." I smile at Koop hoping he doesn't bolt.

"Does Rand know he's there?" Lucas demands.

"No, but . . ."

"Is Angel bringing strange guys back to the room too?" he yells, getting louder.

"Lucas, it's been a real blast talking to you, but I have to go now." I hang up on him before he can interrupt me. I walk over to Angel's wipe-off board hanging above her desk, uncap the marker hanging from it, and write, "Your psycho-possessive boyfriend called."

Koop starts laughing as he reads my message. I sit back down and dig into another slice of pizza.

"So I hear Wynkoop Pharmacueticals is going to save the world," I say. I figure if I get him comfortable talking maybe he'll spill some interesting Mitzi info.

"It's so exciting. Our scientists have developed the only cure for all strains of the avian flu disease," he says, his eyes practically flashing dollar bill signs.

"It sounds like now would be a good time to invest in some WP stock," I joke.

"The best. And I won't even rat you out for the insider information."

I shudder at the thought of an electronic monitoring device being my only accessory for months. I just don't think I could make it work like Martha did.

"I think I'll pass," I tell him.

"It is still in the test stages in Mexico. It hasn't exactly been approved by the FDA yet." I immediately picture some poor Mexican guy in a giant sombrero getting paid one peso to be injected with some strange drug.

"You have the most horrible look on your face, Aspen." Koop laughs. "It's safe. The feds are just giving us a hard time because they know as soon as the drug is approved WP will be the largest pharmaceutical company in the world," he clarifies.

I'm kind of amazed that we are holding a civilized conversation, even if it is about bird flu.

"I don't suppose I can talk you into doing me a favor?" Koop asks, suddenly serious.

"I suppose that depends on what the favor is," I say,

hoping he isn't going to suggest something sexual because then I'll have to kick him out of my room.

"Since you are going to be in the house anyway, I just thought maybe you could try to find out anything you could about Mitzi. We could get together every so often to see what you've found out. Rand doesn't even need to know about it. If you did that for me, I could give you anything you need," he says slyly, wiping pizza grease off his perfectly sculpted chin.

"I've got everything I need, Koop," I respond to his offer. I know now that it was a mistake to try and charm anything out of Koop. He has ulterior motives and I know even giving him an inch could prove to be deadly. Was I crazy? The guy had practically attacked me earlier and I had thought for a second that I could trust him. My blood sugar must be low. I'm about to show him the door when the phone rings again. Damn Lucas.

"Helloooo," I answer, super-annoyed.

"Oh my God, Angel, it's Pippi. Something is wrong with Tobi," Pippi screams into the phone. Why does everybody think Angel is the only one living here?

"Pippi, it's Aspen. What is wrong with Tobi?" I ask calmly.

"I'm not supposed to tell you," Pippi says, suddenly clamming up.

"Spill it, Pippi."

Pippi is Angel's best friend from high school and Tobi's girl lover. On a normal day, I really like her, but today I just want to reach through the phone and shake the information out of her.

"She has an incurable disease," she says sobbing into the phone.

"Pippi, get ahold of yourself. What kind of disease?" I demand.

"It's bird flu." She sobs some more.

A million thoughts spin around my head. I didn't think Tobi even ate chicken. I told Tobi that summer-exchange program in Indonesia was a bad idea. Why does she always refuse to heed my advice? You would think she would know by now that I'm always right.

I hold the phone away from my ear hoping that this is all a very bad dream. I glance at Koop, who is giving me a cocky look, and know that it isn't. The image of a skinnier-than-Kate-Moss Tobi runs through my mind. Now it makes perfect sense why she quit school with no explanation. I hang up the phone without saying good-bye and sink down into my bed, shaking uncontrollably.

"I need your help," I say in a daze, fighting back tears.

"I'll do anything for you, Aspen," he promises, wrapping his arms around me as I sob my guts out.

Six

I hardly slept a wink last night after I found out about Tobi. Koop assured me that he would be on the phone first thing this morning to find out if Wynkoop Pharmaceuticals knows anything about the strain of the disease Tobi has, which is so horrible that I can't even pronounce it. I called her house sobbing last night and her mom told me everything. Tobi was already in bed, which broke my heart. I know she must be super-sick to already be in bed at eleven o'clock. Every college student knows that's when the party is just getting started.

I tiptoe past Angel's bed on my way to the foul community showers. I had pretended to be asleep last night when she came home, even though she did her best to try and wake me up. Her jet black hair makes a spiky halo around her head and black eyeliner is smeared down her face. Her mouth is hanging open quite unattractively and drool has run down her chin and pooled onto her neck. This would be the ultimate blackmail picture but I'm not ready to risk waking her up and having to deal with her wrath over the Betas yet.

I take my time getting ready, loving that this early I have the bathroom all to myself. When I'm done with my makeup and hair, I slip back into our room and put on my favorite jeans and a pink button-down oxford. I slide a headband through my curled hair and grab my purse. I can't help but notice the pile of monogrammed Beta gifts that Angel's sisters got her displayed neatly on her desk.

A tiny streak of jealousy shoots through me as I quietly lock the door and head downstairs to the elevator. My new sisters didn't even let me come to my own stupid party. I knew it was just a control tactic. Cassandra was nothing if not a total control freak and she wanted me to know that she was running the Zeta show. I'll play into her hands as long as it takes to get information about Mitzi for Harry and pacify Koop until Tobi is better, but I won't like it, I think, traipsing across campus to the Zeta house.

There is evidence strewn all over the Greek lawns of the fun had last night. Beer cans, cigarette butts, and pizza boxes litter the perfect emerald lawns. I cringe as I walk by a used condom.

I dart across the Zeta lawn, which is mysteriously absent of any refuse, and pound on the huge wooden door.

A bubbly brunette answers the door. She looks me up and down for a second, a huge smile breaking across her delicate features. I totally blank on her name.

"You don't have to knock, Aspen. You're one of us now." She laughs, ushering me in.

"I wasn't really sure," I say, embarrassed. This whole new girl thing is so not my scene. I really wish I wasn't the only Zeta recruit; it adds a lot of pressure I don't need right now.

She leads me into the great room where all forty of the sisters are sitting. I suddenly feel as if I've been thrown into one of those *Where's Waldo* books. All of my new sisters are dressed casually in gray sweats and mint green Zeta T-shirts. I so didn't get the bulletin that we were all supposed to be dressed like clones. Shit. This does not look good on my first day as an official new member. I hear a collective gasp, and then the room falls silent.

"My bad, I totally forgot to give you your new clothes and outfit alignment sheet," Cassandra says, rushing over to me. The other girls seem to breathe a little easier now that they know it was their fearless leader who made the mistake. I catch the look on Cassandra's face and realize she did it on purpose so that I would make a bad impression my first day.

"Oh, I guess I'll wear these next time," I say, accepting the tote bag Cassandra is thrusting at me.

"You can change in there," she says, pointing to a bathroom in the hall.

All rightee then. Everyone remains silent, staring through me. I see Charm sitting in the back; she raises her hand and smiles. How can someone make sweats and a T-shirt look so good? She's total supermodel material. I move toward the bathroom with forty pairs of eyes on me.

Through the door, I hear the girls start chatting again. They are making a pro and con list to help pick their primary charity for the semester. It's between a breast cancer charity and an organization that makes dreams come true for dying children. From the sounds of it, breast cancer is winning because the girls agree that pink ribbons would be the perfect accessory. I'm cool with anything but Lance Armstrong's charity. If the sisters try to force me to wear one of those tacky-ass Live Strong wristbands, I'll be forced to fake a latex allergy.

I unzip the tote to find a rainbow assortment of Zeta adorned tees, sweats, and tanks. I'm surprised they haven't included Zeta bras and panties. I carefully remove and fold my civilian clothes and slip into the mint green T-shirt and gray sweatpants the other girls are wearing. They are actually quite comfy. As a rule, I don't usually wear sweats. I think wearing clothes with elastic is kind of saying you give up and aren't even going to try and fake a sense of fashion. It's weird that the Zetas have all these tacky outfits when I've seen some of them in Prada and Miu Miu on campus. I guess these outfits are just for hanging out in the house as equals. I can deal with that as long as no one sees me. I slip out of the bathroom and quietly enter the great room.

I hear "Hey, Aspen," about forty times. I smile and take a seat on the floor. Everybody is patting me on the back and acting delighted to see me. It's as if I was invisible in my street clothes, but now that I'm a Zeta clone, I'm one of them again. They probably felt inferior once they saw my impeccable sense of style. I can't say that I blame them.

When the girls ask me which charity I'd pick, I don't even bother making eye contact with the bald-headed, doe-eyed, little boy gazing back at me from the huge laminated Dream Come True poster and say, "That's a no-brainer. Those pink ribbons are to die for." The girls all applaud and squeal with glee, except one who's asleep in a ball on the couch, and we head to the kitchen for snacks to celebrate our good deed.

"So what's the story with Sleepy in there?" I ask Charm, pointing to the girl snoring on the coach.

"Oh, that's Lilly. I think she's got narcolepsy or something. She'll just nod off sometimes. She fell asleep in her dinner plate one night. It was hilarious." She laughs, grabbing a piece of bacon from a tray of meat on the kitchen island.

"Weird." I laugh back while examining Charm from head to toe. I just can't get over how perfect this girl is. And she's nice. It just doesn't add up. When people have looks this good, it is usually compensating for some other defect, but so far I can't find anything wrong with Charm. It's driving me crazy.

"Every sister has to volunteer with a charity. I'm doing a blood drive in a few days. Do you want to help me?" Charm asks.

"What, like take people's blood? Ick!"

"No, silly. We just give out juice and cookies and get people registered." Charm laughs.

"Oh, okay. That doesn't sound too bad." I'm kind of honored that Charm would want to hang out with me and this might be the perfect opportunity to get her talking about Mitzi.

I hear someone banging on the front door and a few of the girls clap their hands together in excitement. Charm flashes me her beyond pearly whites and I just know that I'm about to get a surprise from the Zetas. I bet my surprise will put Angel's monogrammed gifts to shame.

All the sisters rush into the great room and I trail behind. A twenty something guy covered in tats is assembling a massage table in the middle of the room.

"Aspen, come over here," Cassandra tells me as all the other sisters sit cross-legged on the floor.

"Is this her?" the guy asks, giving me the creeps. I stand frozen in my spot. I don't know what kind of a surprise this is but I don't like it.

"Yes, this is our fall recruit, Aspen," Cassandra answers proudly, like I just won her best in show or something.

"Hi, Aspen. I'm Lars. I'm here to give you your body badge," he says kindly.

"Huh?" I snort half-laughing. Badge? Is this the freaking Girl Scouts or what? I hope not because my green sash only had about two badges on it.

"Your body badge. All the sisters have one," Cassandra replies snottily, spinning around and lifting the back of her T-shirt.

"Oh my God, a tattoo!" I shriek, startling Lars and Cassandra. Gasps come up from the sisters on the floor.

"No. Tattoos are for scary white trash. These are body badges, a symbol of our loyalty to our sisters that we will wear forever," Cassandra says, obviously offended, as she turns back to me.

I want to ask her how she thinks she'll feel about her sisters when she's sixty and the bright red heart encasing a thick black Z spreads across her lower back and looks like a wounded zebra crawling to her ass. I wish I could just tell her to shove it and get the heck out of these horrible clothes and house. But I can't. I know that Koop would never keep his end of the bargain if I bailed on mine.

"If you could just remove your shirt and climb on the table, we can get started," Lars says, taking out his tattoo gun.

I have to fight to stay upright. I hate the sight of blood, especially my own. It was bad enough agreeing to give juice and cookies to people with little tubes of blood coming out of their arms. But this is actual pain for yours truly. Not to mention that I'll be left with a skanky tattoo on my backside for all of eternity. I can't do this.

"All the sisters have badges. If you want to be a sister, you have to get one," Cassandra spouts. It's like she wants us all to be branded like a bunch of cattle or something. I'm quickly developing an intense hatred for Cassandra.

"Okay," I say, climbing onto the table, "but I should warn you. I'm a bleeder." I smile brightly then lay on the table with the back of my T-shirt flipped up.

"You're a hemophiliac?" Lars asks in horror.

"Yep, if I get so much as a scrape, I practically have to have a blood transfusion."

"Oh, hell no," Lars says, packing up his equipment. I sit up and pull down my shirt, trying not to smile smugly in Cassandra's direction.

"How convenient," she says disgusted. "Since Aspen can't show her loyalty to her sisters by getting a body badge then we'll need to think of some other way for people to know she is our recruit," she says, tapping her fingers on her chin evilly.

"She could wear a sign around all the time," someone from the back shouts.

Yeah, as if!

"That's a great idea. Our letter is our sign. Aspen, you are no longer permitted to wear civilian clothes during your initiation period. You will only wear the Zeta-monogrammed clothes I gave you today," Cassandra says happily, her eyes challenging me.

⊙

"She doesn't mean to be such a bitch," Charm says, striding alongside me with a gigantic backpack slung on her shoulder. It's midafternoon and Charm is walking to the library and I'm heading back to the dorm.

"You could have fooled me," I answer back.

"She's just stressed. She was really close to Mitzi and I guess maybe she sees you as her replacement."

"Am I?" I ask, horrified.

"Of course not. Don't be silly," she says, not meeting my eyes.

"What do you think happened to her?" I ask, stopping in front of the library.

"I wish I could tell you," she says, turning to walk into the library.

"Hey, Charm," I yell stopping her. "Do you think her boyfriend might have had something to do with her disappearing?"

She shakes her head violently, and then replies, "Mitzi didn't have a boyfriend."

After saying good-bye to Charm, I book back to my dorm room to drop off my very uncouturelike new Zeta wardrobe. I peel out of the Zeta sweats and get back into my jeans and shirt. I feel human again. Screw Cassandra and her rules.

"If it isn't Little Miss Zeta," Angel smarts off, coming

in the door with a towel around her wet hair and one wrapped around her petite frame.

"Angel, I'm sorry. They were just a better fit," I lie. I don't want to involve Angel in my undercover work because I know she would try to get right in the middle of it. This whole thing is a big enough mess without putting Angel in danger.

"Whatever," she says, whipping the towel off.

"Excuse me," I say, shielding my eyes.

"Oh, that's right. We're not close enough to be naked in front of each other. We'd have to be sisters for that and we weren't meant to be sisters, were we, Aspen?"

She slips a long T-shirt over her body then dissolves into a mess of tears on her bed.

"Angel, we don't have to be sorority sisters to be friends," I say, trying to comfort her.

"You aren't my friend," she says, through her sobs.

"Yes, I am, whether you like it or not," I demand. "What about Pippi, isn't she still your friend?" I ask.

"Yeah, so?" she says, sitting up and wiping her nose on the end of her shirt.

"She's not even in the same town but that doesn't make her any less of a friend, does it?"

"No, I guess not," she says, wiping her face on her shirt. "That really bites about Tobi," she says, changing the subject. Pippi must have called her this morning while I was at the Zeta house.

"Tobi's going to be just fine," I respond positively.

Angel gives me a surprised look. "Angel, there is something you need to know about me. There is nothing I won't do for my friends."

As soon as I calm Angel down, I head downstairs to Rand and Koop's room. I take the steps slowly remembering how positive Charm was that Mitzi didn't have a boyfriend. How could you live in the same room with someone and not know everything that was going on with them? It's not possible. That means that Koop lied, but why?

I pound on the outer door and a chubby redhead lets me in. I walk the now-familiar path to their room hoping maybe they are getting along a little better now. I feel positively guilty over collapsing into Koop's arms, but I was so distraught and I know that Rand will understand. Not that I'd be volunteering the information but it wouldn't surprise me if Koop slipped it in somehow. Rand doesn't even know that Koop used to date Mitzi, well, maybe, or that Tobi is sick. He's been at the Nu house so much I haven't had time to fill him in.

When I get to their door it is already half open. They are both lying on their beds, ignoring each other.

"Aspen!" they both yell simultaneously. Talk about your awkward moment.

"What happened to your eye?" I shout, taking in the black and blue swelling around Rand's left eye.

"It looks worse than it is," he says, wincing as he touches it.

"I told you those Nus were nothing but trouble," Koop adds, leaning up on his elbow. He has one leg bent and is wearing a pair of camo cargo pants. The shorts are gaping and I can see straight down to his boy part. After seeing it, I immediately look away, embarrassed. It isn't lost on Koop. He laughs and slides his leg straight down on the bed. I take a minute to get my breath after that unexpected, but not entirely unpleasant, sight.

"Piss off, Sam," Rand yells.

"Rand, what is he talking about?" I move to sit down next to Rand.

"It's just Nu tradition. The Nus line up all the pledges and everyone has to recite the Greek alphabet backward. If anybody screws up, everybody gets punched."

"Oh my God." I recoil in horror.

"I tried to tell him," Koop says smugly.

"Shut up," both Rand and I yell in his direction. He throws us a dirty look, grabs his cell, and leaves.

"Thank God," Rand says, running a hand through his curls as he lies back down.

"That really is horrible, Rand." I trace his black eye with my fingertip. I hated the thought of someone being mean to him for no reason. Then I remember Cassandra and how she had it out for me and I wonder if almost being forced to get a tattoo or wearing ugly clothes is just as bad as being punched.

I thought going Greek was going to be the best time of our lives but so far it had been a total nightmare. How had we gotten ourselves into this big fat Greek mess?

"I hate that guy," Rand says, pulling me close to him.

"About that, Rand. We kind of need him."

"What are you talking about?" he asks, jerking upright.

"It turns out that he may have used to date Mitzi," I say, bracing for Rand's explosion.

"He killed her. I know he did. It makes perfect sense," Rand mumbles, staring off into space.

"Um, I don't think so." Koop strikes me as a lot of things, but a cold-blooded killer isn't one of them.

"I've gotta get a room transfer," Rand says, jumping off the bed.

"It's more complicated than that, Rand. Something is wrong with Tobi. Koop has promised to help her if I help find out what happened to Mitzi."

"No, absolutely not. This is getting serious, Aspen. We're not talking about a demented homecoming queen this time. This is a billionaire's son who possibly killed his girlfriend. People with that much money can cover anything up." He lays his hands on my shoulders and gazes into my eyes with genuine worry.

"There is something going on in that sorority house, Rand. I can feel it. I have to do this for Tobi and for Harry."

"Will I ever be able to boss you around?" Rand asks, defeated.

"Very doubtful," I say, clasping my arms around his neck and kissing his bad eye.

"I really hate it when you use your lips to get your way," he says, leaning into my lips.

"No, you don't," I manage to get out before melting into Rand's luscious lips.

The room is dark when I wake up. I roll over and hear a piece of paper crunch beneath me. Rand's bedside clock says it's eight o'clock already. I rub my eyes and try to shake the confusion from my head. Could this really be the same day? I feel like I've been asleep for days. I switch on Rand's lamp and pull the piece of paper from underneath me. It's a note from Rand.

Had to go to the house. I'll be back soon. Be careful. I love you.

I fold up the note and stick it in my jeans pocket. I always keep any note that Rand ever writes me, even if it's on a Post-It. I'm a real girl like that.

I push myself off Rand's bed and start walking in the space between his and Koop's beds. Someone's backpack is tossed in the middle of the floor. I scoot around it and my foot scrapes against something under Koop's bed.

"Holy crap," I yell, pulling my foot out. Blood gushes

from a three-inch scrape down the center of my foot. I feel under the bed to find what I could have cut my foot on. I pull out a sterling silver box with four razor-sharp edges. The lid is embossed with some type of crest of arms.

I pop the top to find it empty except for a medium-sized Tiffany box. I know I should put it back, but what girl can resist opening a Tiffany jewelry box? Carefully I slide the blue lid off to find a sterling silver bangle bracelet resting on fluffy white gauze. The engraving reads, *Mitzi*. So Koop wasn't lying after all. He must have bought this for Mitzi but didn't get to give it to her before she disappeared. I am surprised at how bad I feel for him. To have someone you love just disappear off the face of the earth. I know now that even if Tobi weren't sick I'd still keep up my end of our bargain.

"Do you think she would have liked it?" Koop's deep voice booms, causing me to dump the box and the bracelet with a squeal.

"I wasn't spying, really. I just cut my foot on this thing and it came flying out from under the bed," I explain, holding up my bloody foot as evidence.

"It's okay, Aspen. I don't have anything to hide. I'm glad you found it," he says, walking to his closet and returning with some antibiotic cream and a bandage for my foot.

I put the bracelet back into the box as delicately as possible. My eyes linger on the engraving for a minute. What a waste of Tiffany jewelry.

"So do you think she would have liked it?" he asks, returning with the first-aid supplies.

"What girl wouldn't?" I answer, wondering why he always refers to Mitzi in past tense.

"What kind of jewelry do you like, Aspen?" he asks, sitting on the edge of the bed pulling my leg toward him.

What a weird question, I think, and then I realize he's probably just trying to distract me while he cleans my foot.

"I'm an emerald girl. I think they are so exotic. Someday I'd like at least a two carat emerald for my engagement ring," I giggle, giddy talking about jewels.

"That's a good choice. My dad owns some emerald fields in Colombia," he adds, dabbing some ointment on my foot.

"Ouch, that burns," I say, pulling my foot away. He takes it back and rests my foot against his chest then starts blowing on it, instantly stopping the stinging.

"Do you know why Mitzi's roommate wouldn't know she had a boyfriend?" I ask, trying to shock him into tripping up if he is lying.

"The Zetas didn't know. No one knew. Mitzi knew they wouldn't approve of her dating a GDI. She was afraid of being kicked out of the sorority," he answers, without the least bit of hesitation. That sealed it for me: Koop was telling the truth. I felt sorry for Charm that she hadn't really even known her roommate and the girl she was mourning.

"I should go," I say, pushing myself off the bed.

"Not yet," Koop says, pulling me back down. For a second our faces are dangerously close together then he swings my legs across his lap and gently takes my injured foot and puts a bandage on it.

I am still reeling at bit when the door flies open and Rand stumbles in. His glassy eyes take in my feet across Koop's lap, and he seems to stop breathing for a second. I jump off the bed, even though it hurts really bad, and hobble over to him.

"I hurt my foot and Koop was just helping me," I explain. The last thing I need tonight is to break up a fist-fight between these two. I wrap my arms around Rand's neck and lean in to kiss him. I am immediately assaulted with his one-hundred-proof breath.

"Are you drunk?" I shout in shock.

"No," he answers, then promptly falls to the floor and passes out.

"Rand!" I shriek, trying to hold him up. Koop rushes over, scoops Rand up and deposits him on his bed. Rand doesn't even flinch.

"What the hell? Rand doesn't drink," I say, rolling him onto his side in case he throws up.

"It must have been pledge shot night. The Nus always have a night where all the new pledges have to drink a shot for every pledge in their class," Koop explains, taking a seat on his own bed.

I vaguely remember Rand mentioning thirteen pledges in his class when I told him that I was the only Zeta.

"Oh my God!" I say, realizing just how annihilated Rand must be. Just then Rand starts laughing hysterically for no apparent reason but never opens his eyes. After a few seconds, he quiets down and starts snoring peacefully.

Koop and I exchange a giggle. I lay down behind Rand and stroke his sweat-soaked hair. There is no way I'm leaving him alone tonight. I prop myself up on my elbow so that I can talk to Koop.

"You're a good girlfriend," Koop says, watching me stroke Rand's curls.

"I'm worried about him. He doesn't do things like this," I confess.

"He's just trying to fit in, like you with the Zetas. You guys aren't the big fish of Comfort High anymore."

Boy, was I starting to realize that. Last year, I ruled the school. When Rand and I walked the halls, people would magically make a path and stare in awe as we passed. But at State, nobody cares who we are or where we came from. Talk about getting knocked off your pedestal.

"You'll get hazed just like Rand. They just don't have you drinking shots," Koop continues. I think of the bag of horrendous sweat outfits and know he is right.

"What did you find out about helping Tobi?" I ask, changing the subject. If I'm going to be stuck here with a passed-out boyfriend and his slightly sadistic roommate, I'm not going to waste time with chitchat.

"I've arranged for Tobi and her family to be taken to Mexico so that she can begin treatment. She'll have to be kept there for several weeks so that her progress can be tracked," he says.

Relief floods my exhausted body. I know it isn't a promise that Tobi will get better, but it's the best I can do.

"What can you tell me about these sorority sisters of mine?" I ask, hoping that he can shed the light on some of the Zetas' shady behavior.

"Let's see. They'll make you get a tattoo," he says, trying to shock me.

"Oh, I so got out of that."

"Aspen, you amaze me. Is there anyone you can't charm to get your way?"

My cell rings and I grab it out of my pocket and answer it before it can wake Rand up.

"Aspen? There is some guy here in a limo who says he's going to fly me and my parents out of the country on a private jet. He says you sent him," Tobi's voice says nervously, still half-asleep.

"Go with him, Tobi. He's going to make sure you get better," I tell her, praying I'm right. Koop gets off his bed and turns his back to me. He slips his shirt over his head to reveal a tanned, muscular back. Before I can look away, he drops his camo cargos. His ass looks like it is carved out of marble. I can barely breathe. He jumps into his bed and thankfully doesn't face me, as I'm sure my mouth is hanging wide open.

"What? Yes, I'm still here," I tell Tobi. I see Koop shaking with laughter at the effect he knows he had on me. I would never cheat on Rand in a million years but it is impossible not to drool over Koop a little bit. People don't usually realize it, but I'm only human.

"Aspen, how did you do this?" Tobi pleads.

"It doesn't matter. You need to focus on getting better and nothing else because I can't lose you."

Tobi and I exchange tearful good-byes and I slip my phone back into my jeans pocket. I curl into Rand's back, hoping he doesn't wake up and puke in my hair. I close my eyes and try to stop seeing Koop's amazing ass.

Seven

After showering the next morning, I slip into a clean pair of Zeta sweats. The yellow of the material makes me look jaundiced, I think, looking in the mirror on the back of our door. I have an almost overwhelming urge to take a pair of scissors to all of the horrible outfits. But then Cassandra would kick me out of the Zetas and I wouldn't be able to figure out what happened to Mitzi and help Tobi. I wonder if my friends appreciate the sacrifices I make for them. I highly doubt it.

"So last night we had a pizza party and gave each other manis and pedis. Then we watched chick flicks all night. Did you see the stuff my big sister, Betsy, gave me?" Angel rambles on, stopping only to turn up her nose upon seeing my outfit. "You shouldn't wear yellow," she tells me, as if I didn't already know this.

It's cool that she is so happy about being a Beta, but do I have to hear every teensy detail? When our dorm phone rings, I'm thankful that she'll have to stop talking for a second.

"Don't answer it," Angel says seriously, hovering near the phone like she's ready to pound me if I reach for it.

"Why not?" I ask, moving toward it.

"It's probably Lucas, and I'm not ready to talk to him," she says, puffing up her chest as if to warn me.

"I could so take you." I laugh. "What is going on with you two anyway?" I shout over the phone.

"I don't know," she answers. When the phone finally stops ringing, she stares at it, looking sad.

My cell phone immediately starts ringing and I pick it up to check the display. I'm not shocked to see that Lucas is the one calling. Angel must be keeping her cell phone off so Lucas is using his only other option. He sure wasn't as persistent when we were dating!

"Figure it out," I tell her, turning my phone off. The last thing I need right now is to be sandwiched in between Angel and Lucas. I have way too much other stuff to deal with right now, like trying not to gag when I have to help Charm hand out juice and cookies to people voluntarily having their blood taken. Gag!

I'm looking forward to seeing Charm today, I just wish it were under different circumstances. I guess it's cool that the Zetas help out in the community although I suspect they probably have ulterior motives for just about everything they do. I figure Charm and I will have plenty of time to chat. I mean, how many people actually donate blood anyway?

I push through the doors of the Student Center to be met with a huge crowd. Tons of people of all ages are actually standing in line waiting to be victimized, I mean, have their blood taken. I can't believe it. You'd think they were actually paying them to give blood or something. I make my way through the crowd to the head of the line. Charm looks a little frazzled as she tries to arrange people by blood types.

"Need some help?" I ask, startling her. A look of pure relief comes over her face as she slips a badge over my neck that reads "Volunteer."

"I'm so glad you are here. Can you start handing out cups of juice and cookies to all of the people wearing the 'I gave blood' stickers?" she asks, pointing to her own sticker.

"No problem." I smile, breezing past the desk and over to a table holding several gallon jugs of orange juice and unopened packages of cookies. I open the cookies and start arranging them on a platter then do the same with Dixie cups full of juice. I balance both trays on the palms of my hands and make the rounds through the room. The donors accept the refreshments gratefully and I'm ecstatic that no one seems to be on the verge of collapse.

"Would you like a refill, sir?" I ask an old man on my second round through the lounge.

"You're not Mitzi," he grumbles, crumpling up his Dixie cup.

"No, I'm not. Did you know Mitzi?" I ask, curious.

"Mitzi always got me apple juice. She's prettier than you," he says, shoving an entire cookie in his mouth.

"It's the outfit," I explain. "Was she here a lot?"

"She always gets her blood taken when I do. She's my girlfriend," he says confidently.

Sure, buddy, whatever. Wow, so Mitzi had two boyfriends that Charm didn't know about. Okay, so now I know that Mitzi was a total saint for putting up with this guy and getting her blood taken. I really hope Charm doesn't expect me to give blood because that so was not part of the deal.

"She's nicer than you," he says, giving me a dirty look.

"No more cookies for you," I tell him, whisking away with the platter. Nobody insults Aspen Brooks and gets away with it, not even an elderly blood donor.

"Aspen, you're a lifesaver," Charm interrupts.

"I love volunteer work," I lie with a smile.

"There is a group of girls getting their blood taken

together over there. Can you make sure they get a sticker?" she asks, handing me the roll of stickers.

"Oh, sure." I drop off the cookies and head toward a group of college-age girls. As I get closer I realize they are all Betas. They are sitting together in a big group giggling even though tiny tubes are draining blood out of their arms into plastic pouches. Angel sits in the middle surrounded by a few other girls. I recognize some of them from the recruitment party. I'm surprised by the flicker of jealousy I feel seeing these other girls bonding with Angel. It's not that I don't want her to have other friends. I guess I just wish I were bonding with them, but not over getting my blood taken!

"Hey, everybody. I just need to give you a sticker," I say, passing them out.

"Aspen, I wondered what sorority you went with. We really thought you were a Beta girl," the Beta who was my party escort says. I shrug my shoulders, not really knowing what to say. Deep down, I know I'm a Beta girl too.

"Hey, roomie," Angel says, weakly, as I put a sticker on her pink Beta tee. I can't believe the sisters actually got her to wear something that isn't black.

"How's it going over here?" Charm asks, coming up behind me.

"Good. I'm just giving my roomie a sticker." I laugh, eliciting a smile from a pale Angel. I'm thinking that the whole blood donation thing wasn't her idea. "Angel, this is Charm. Charm, this is Angel."

"Hey," Angel says, smiling at Charm.

"I didn't know your roommate was a Beta," Charm says, almost accusingly. Her tone isn't lost on Angel either who gives me a strange look. "I bet she's really going to miss you when you move into the Zeta house," Charm finishes, smiling almost wickedly, as I stand, stunned. Angel shoots death looks from her overly made up eyes.

"That's really great, Aspen," Angel says, in a fake syrupy voice.

"Angel, I didn't . . ." I start to say but Charm interrupts me.

"I think those people over there need stickers," Charm says, pointing to the opposite side of the room. I head that way, avoiding Angel's eyes.

☉

As I distribute juice and cookies the rest of the day, I can't help but think how weird it will be to move into the Zeta house. I despise the concrete jungle but I love that Rand only lives a few steps away. And even though Angel has only been my roomie for a few days, I am comfortable living with her. We have fun and I'll miss her. But I guess if I am really going to immerse myself in this investigation I need to get as close to the Zetas as possible.

"You can take off if you want," Charm says, walking up as I tear open the last bag of cookies. The crowd has died down considerably and she could easily handle things by herself.

"I think I will," I say, knowing that I have to hunt down Angel and try to make her understand that I didn't know about my impending move. "Why didn't anyone tell me that I was going to be moving into the Zeta house?"

"What do you mean?" she asks, looking innocent.

"It just kind of felt like you ambushed me in front of my roommate. I didn't like it." I was only willing to put up with so much from the Zetas and they needed to know it. I was willing to be pushed a bit, but not shoved.

"I guess maybe seeing you with her made me a little bit jealous. The Betas are so cliquey and they have a way of stealing our members," she admits.

"I'm not going anywhere, but next time, let me decide when to share information about my own life. Okay?"

Charm nods her head yes and I bolt out the door. I'm not really upset with her anymore but I couldn't take looking at the nasty blood pouches being packed in their special coolers for one more second. I'm all for saving lives and all that but does it have to be so gross?

I push through the doors to the quad and see Angel waiting for me. It looks like I'm being the one hunted down instead.

"Thanks for the four-one-one on your living situation. I knew you didn't want to room with me but you could have at least given it a week," she says, big tears forming in her black-lined eyes.

"I like living with you, Angel," I tell her.

She rolls her eyes and starts walking away. "Now I've heard it all," she says.

"What? I really do. For right now I have to do everything they want. It won't always be like this," I say, trying to make her understand without giving anything away.

"Of course it will. They are trying to control you and doing a pretty good job. They tell you where to live, who to be friends with, and what to wear," she says, pointing distastefully at my outfit.

"No one controls me. You should know that better than anyone, Angel."

"I just don't get it," she says, shaking her head. I feel so bad that I can't tell her the truth, that I don't like the Zetas anymore than she does, but I just can't yet.

"Just think, now you and Lucas can get your freak on when he comes to visit without having to worry about me walking in on you," I tell her, laughing.

She kicks an empty water bottle with her Sketchers and it flies toward a squirrel. It turns and stalks up to us as if to start a confrontation. The squirrels on this campus are totally psycho. We get an all-campus e-mail about someone getting bit at least once a week.

"Lucas doesn't love me like he loved you." Angel blubbers, distracting me from the squirrel. I turn toward her tear-soaked face and hear a high-pitched squeak. I look down at my Nike and see that I've impaled the squirrel's bushy tale under my shoe. I scream and lift my foot. The squirrel takes off across campus leaving a pile of reddish-brown hair behind.

"Tell your friends," I shout after him. He turns, and for just a second, I contemplate running. Then he scurries up a tree. I'm not normally so skittish around furry little animals but I don't need a raging cage of rabies right now with everything else I'm dealing with.

I look back toward Angel expecting her to still be crying, but she's doubled over laughing hysterically.

"You didn't know I was feared by squirrels, did you?" I say, hugging her. "Now let's get the hell out of here before he comes back with his friends."

⊙

Angel and I stop at the local coffeehouse. I get a hot chocolate because I so don't do coffee. We sink down into one of the comfy velvet couches for a chat.

"Why were you talking that smack about Lucas? He totally loves you," I say, blowing on my hot chocolate.

"I don't know, I just think he's going to get tired of me and dump me, so I figure I'll dump him first," she replies, adding six teaspoonfuls of sugar to her black coffee.

"Oh, that's mature. What makes you think he'll dump you anyway?"

"They always do, eventually. I just figure it'll hurt less now than in twenty years," she answers, fidgeting with her cell phone.

"Lucas isn't your dad, Angel. You can't punish him for someone else's mistake," I tell her, reaching out to touch her hand.

She looks up with tears in her eyes and nods. My cell rings totally interrupting our Hallmark moment, but it's Rand, so it's worth it.

"Are you still hungover?" I answer.

Angel mouths, "What?" and I nod to affirm that my straight-arrow boyfriend did indeed tie one or thirteen on last night.

"Are you mad?" Rand asks, sounding pitiful.

"Not mad, just confused. I thought you were joining a frat to make friends, not get drunk and have people beat you up," I say, then immediately feel like a hypocrite.

"Do you want me to quit?" he asks.

"Only if you want to," I say, then immediately regret it. If he's a GDI, he won't be acceptable dating material, at least to the Zetas, so we'll have to sneak around to see each other.

"I really don't. I like these guys. I'll just start telling them when I'm not comfortable doing something."

"That sounds like a plan. How about dinner tonight? We haven't hardly seen each other all week," I whine.

Angel twirls a short piece of hair with one hand while making gagging motions with the other. I kindly flip her off, a gesture she is very familiar with from me.

"I can't. We've got mandatory study tonight."

"But it's Saturday! That's so lame."

"I know, I'm sorry. You know I'd rather be with you," he says in a sexy voice, making me really wish we could be together tonight.

"I guess I'll just hang at the dorm tonight then," I say, beyond disappointed.

We exchange "love yous," and promise to meet up to-morrow.

"Why didn't you tell him about the move?" Angel asks.

The girl picks up on everything. I knew that Rand's re-action would be even worse than Angel's and it wasn't something I wanted to do over the phone. I'll tell him to-morrow, which will still give him plenty of time to get used to the idea before I actually move out.

"I want to tell him in person," I reply, and then take a huge swig of hot chocolate.

"His head is going to explode," Angel says knowingly.

"I think you have enough boyfriend problems of your own to worry about. You leave Rand to me." She nods in agreement, knowing I'm right.

She spends the next fifteen minutes telling me about the fun night the Betas have planned for the pledges with-out taking a breath. I love that she's found a sorority to fit in to but it's so hard not to be jealous. Tobi's face flashes in my mind and the jealousy quickly dissipates. I know that every fun night I'm sacrificing is worth it to get her well again.

Angel and I catch up on the Comfort gossip we've both heard from our parents since we've been gone as we walk to our dorm. It doesn't sound like I've missed much although I do really miss my parents.

We open the heavy steel door to our floor and walk down the corridor to our room. I grimace looking at the horribly outdated furnishings. Maybe living in the Zeta mansion won't be that bad.

"Just don't let them start controlling you," Angel says, sliding her badge into our door lock.

"As if!" I laugh, pushing the door open.

My eyes notice a difference in the room immediately but it takes a few seconds for my brain to catch up. Once it does I realize that everything I own is gone.

"What was that you were saying?" Angel smarts off. I stand frozen to the floor with my mouth gaping open in disbelief.

☺

I'm not even going to lie. Once the shock wore off, I was beyond miffed that my stuff was gone. I barely know these girls and they just come in to my personal space and hijack my stuff. I swear, if my cashmere V-neck has even one crease in it, somebody is going to pay. I am huffing my way over to the house now to give the sisters a piece of my mind.

I'm halfway to the house when my phone beeps that I have a text message. I pull it from my purse and stop in the middle of the quad to check it. It's from Rand and reads, "*Meet me at Marinara, ASAP.*"

Suddenly I could not care less about the sisters U-Hauling my stuff to the Zeta house. I'll deal with them later. I'm just ecstatic that Rand got out of his study session early. I look down at my nasty jaundice sweat suit and groan. This is so not dinner attire. I can't go to the house to change because I'm not supposed to be wearing civilian clothes. Ugh!

But . . . Angel and I are the same size and I know she'll let me borrow something. We might not have the same taste in clothes but I'll take anything over these rags. I rush back to the dorm catching her just on her way out.

"Did you quit the Zetas?" she asks, excitedly.

"No, I didn't make it there. I need something to wear. Rand texted me to meet him for dinner," I say, out of breath.

"I just got this new dress that you'll look smokin' in," she says, pulling me into the room. She opens her closet and grabs an adorable Betsey Johnson dress I saw in one of my magazines. I can hardly believe it when she hands it to me. The tags haven't even been cut off yet. I wouldn't let another soul touch this dress, and she is just giddy about me wearing it. It doesn't escape me that I'm very lucky to have a friend like Angel.

"Wow, Angel. Thanks," I say, ripping off my sweats and slipping into the dress. It clings to my curves like a glove. Angel slides the most adorable pair of matching heels to me. I slide into them and they fit perfectly.

"You look incredible." She smiles, proud that she could help me. I redo my makeup, fix my hair a little bit, and borrow some perfume before heading out.

"You're a good friend, Angel Ives," I say, smiling at her. She puts her hand to her chest and I can tell what I said means the world to her. Our dorm phone starts ringing and Angel's smile falls.

"Answer it, Angel. He loves you," I say, and then run as fast as I can in heels down the stairs to the elevators.

I send Rand a text message that I am on my way when I'm in the elevator so I know he won't leave, but I still haul it across campus as fast as I can because I can't wait to see him.

I'm crossing the street when I feel someone watching me. A white car pulls up next to me and I see the passenger side window being lowered out of the corner of my eye. I pick up the pace a little and act like I don't notice. I keep my hand on the zipper of my purse just in case I need to pull out my whistle.

"Aspen," a deep voice yells from inside the car. I'm so not falling for that. Just because he knows my name doesn't mean he knows me. State sends out a yearbook with pictures of the new freshmen so he might just be a stalker, which on any other day might be kind of a compliment, but today, I just don't have time.

The car speeds up and moves closer to the sidewalk. I

quickly glance over and see hair. Tons and tons of hair. Am I being stalked by a driving werewolf?

"Aspen, stop, it's Harry," the voice yells.

Harry? I stop and look inside the car. It's a hairier version of Harry with a full-grown beard. Hadn't I just seen him like a week ago? How is it even possible to grow a beard in a week? I have a feeling those poor little girls of his are going to be very familiar with electrolysis when they get a little bigger. He props open the passenger door and I slide in.

"Give me a freaking heart attack, why don't you?" I yell, trying to act serious and not crack up at his appearance. "Nice accessory, by the way," I say, pointing to his beard.

He strokes his beard with one hand and smiles. "Really? You like it?" he asks, his eyes wide.

"Um, no. I was being sarcastic." I roll my eyes at him.

"What are you doing walking alone on campus at night?" he demands, suddenly angry.

"What are you doing stalking me out of your jurisdiction?"

"Don't be cute, Aspen. I've seen you leaving the Zeta house."

Busted. I so don't need this. As if I don't have enough stress, now Harry is going to be all in my face about not listening to him.

"I don't know why you do the things you do, but I'm really glad." He beams, totally throwing me off.

"Huh?" I ask, confused.

"You really enjoy undercover work, don't you?"

I had never really thought about it, but I guess I do. I liked figuring out answers to questions most people think are unsolvable. Even though I haven't gotten too deep into Mitzi's disappearance, I know that soon I will be and I'm looking forward to it.

"You are so much like me," Harry says with a grin.

I hold up a hand to disagree. "What exactly are you smoking?" I ask him.

"I never could have asked you to put yourself in danger, but now that you've infiltrated the house, I can finally get our family some answers."

"Whoa, easy boy. I haven't infiltrated anything. They came and moved my stuff into the house today without me even knowing about it. Most of these chicks seem a little controlling but I really don't think there is a killer running around in a Zeta sweatshirt," I say, not wanting Harry to get his hopes up.

"Any clues are better than what we've had."

"Harry, I really want to help you find Mitzi, but you need to know that I'm doing this to help Tobi too. There is a guy who goes to school here that can help her. His family owns Wynkoop Pharmaceuticals. But I have to give him any information I find about Mitzi too."

"Why does he want information about Mitzi?" Harry asks, confused. I guess that answers my next question about whether or not Harry's family knew about Koop. I got why Mitzi kept Koop a secret from the Zetas, but why would she keep him a secret from her own family?

"They were dating when she disappeared," I tell him gently, knowing I'm dropping a bomb.

"Wait, what? I always thought . . . Well, that doesn't matter now, but the campus police never said anything about questioning a boyfriend," he says, outraged.

"I don't think Mitzi told anyone about him for some reason. The Zetas for sure didn't know."

"He could be dangerous. He could have killed her and now you're making deals with him?"

"He wants to find her just as much as we do," I answer.

"This feels wrong, Aspen. Why would Mitzi keep him a secret from everyone?" He grips the steering wheel in frustration. I know it is driving him crazy that he can't be more involved in the investigation since State is way out of his jurisdiction but part of me is glad. He is way too close to this case.

"You're going to have to trust me. Rand knows everything so nothing is going to happen to me." At least not if Rand is sober and not attending some fight club when I need him, but I don't mention this to Harry.

"I'll call you when I know anything," I say, nervously glancing at the glowing blue digits on Harry's dashboard.

"Hot date?" he asks, noticing my sudden fidgeting.

"You could say that." I laugh.

"I'll drive you," he says, pulling away from the curb. I direct him toward Marinara and slouch back to enjoy the ride.

"I'm glad you and Rand are together. That boy's got a good head on his shoulders. He's a keeper," Harry informs me, as if I didn't already know this.

"It's really different here," I answer back, thinking of the past week and how much Rand and I have already been seperated.

"You guys are the real thing, kid. Don't forget that." He pulls up to the restaurant and I jump out, ready to spend a romantic evening with Rand.

"Aspen?" Harry asks, stopping me. I duck my head down in the car to look at him. "Please tell Angel to call Lucas. He called me earlier demanding that I put out an APB on her." He laughs. I nod and wave at him before disappearing into the restaurant.

Eight

"Are you Aspen?" asks a blonde so tiny that she can barely see over the wood podium she's standing behind.

"The one and only," I respond, breathless with anticipation of my evening with Rand.

"Cool. Follow me," she says, stepping from behind the podium and leading me through the main dining area. I smooth down Angel's dress while scanning tables for Rand. I follow the blonde into a back room tucked away from the other diners. I should have known that Rand would make this as special as possible. The blonde leads me to a private room lit only by candlelight, making it nearly impossible to make out anything but a silhouette seated at a small round table in the center of the room. I can see the outline of a large bouquet of flowers in the middle of the table. Light jazz plays in the background and the whole scene is so romantic I could die.

"Thanks, I'll take it from here," I tell the hostess.

"You're a lucky girl. He's on fire," she tells me, then reluctantly turns to go giving Rand one last glance. I fluff my hair one last time and shake off the jealousy vibe that her comment stirred up. Who can blame her? Rand is all that. He is more important to me than any sorority, undercover work, or GPA, and I plan to spend the entire evening proving that to him.

The scent of his new cologne is intoxicating. He must have bought it special just for tonight. It's going to my head quick.

"Oh, the things I'm going to do to you," I tell him.

"You can do anything you want to me," a strange voice says back. The flame on one of the candles flickers brightly across his features. Only they aren't Rand's.

"You! What are you doing here and where is Rand?" I ask in shock.

"I don't know. With his brothers, I guess. Personally I think he's crazy for choosing them over you," Koop says, getting up and pulling out my chair.

"He asked me to meet him here."

"Guilty," Koop says, taking Rand's cell phone from his pocket. I grab it out of his hand.

"You stole Rand's phone?" I yell.

"He left it in the room and I didn't have your number

so I figured I'd just text you," he says smoothly, easing me down into my chair.

"And you just happened to send the text from Rand's phone instead of just taking my number off his phone book?" I ask, furious. Leave it to Koop to pull a dumb-ass stunt like this. I was so looking forward to spending a quiet dramaless evening with Rand.

"I just wanted to have dinner with you," Koop says, as I stand to leave, "to talk about Mitzi. I miss her so much," he says, looking away from me.

Oh, hell. What do I have to lose? It's not like I had anything to do tonight anyway and I'm starving. The worst that could happen is that I get free dinner and some Mitzi information.

"All right, but you better not start talking shit about Rand or I'm outta here," I warn him, sitting back down. I know Rand would be crazy jealous if he knew I was here with Koop but if I blow Koop off he might decide to put Tobi right back on a plane to Comfort. I know that he is used to getting his way and that I can only push him so far, which really sucks.

A thirtysomething waitress comes to take our order and doesn't even raise an eyebrow when Koop orders a bottle of wine with our dinner.

"I'll just have ice water with my dinner," I tell her, even though she hasn't taken her eyes off Koop long enough to take my order. I have no interest in drinking with Koop. I am smart enough to know that I need all of my brain cells functioning on high alert to deal with him.

"So, tell me how you met Mitzi?" I ask, once the waitress stops drooling long enough to drop off our salads.

Koop looks up, surprised, and then lowers his fork. "We met at the gym," he answers.

Part of me wonders, by the shady way he is acting, if he even remembers. Men are so pathetic when it comes to important details, except for Rand of course. I bet Koop could tell me about the first time they had sex in photographic detail though.

"You remind me of her a lot. Especially your hair," Koop says, reaching over to touch my perfectly coiffed locks. I smack his hand to keep him from messing it up. What a weird thing to say anyway; Mitzi has dark brown hair, not blond, like mine. Maybe she got highlights before her untimely demise.

"Sorry, it's just hard sometimes. I beat myself up a lot wondering if there is something I could have done to help her," he says, lowering his eyes.

He looks so incredibly pathetic that I decide to change the subject. I've got all night to pump him for Mitzi info.

"So, is the food any good here?"

"It's pathetic compared to authentic Italian cuisine," he answers snottily. "I'll fly you to Capri for dinner someday."

Oh, yeah, you, me, and your daddy's private jet, that's

gonna happen. Not! I smile but don't respond. A flash of anger crosses Koop's features as he realizes I have no intention of ever flying to another country with him. Could Mitzi have done something to bring out his angry streak?

"What's the deal with you and Rand-bo anyway?" he asks, changing the subject, his face devoid of any anger now.

"We've been together for almost a year now. There's really not much to tell. We're in love," I answer, bubbling with pride.

"That's sweet," Koop says, but looks ready to gag on a breadstick. "What do you love about him?"

"Everything," I answer easily.

Luckily we get interrupted by the arrival of our entrees. I am so not comfortable discussing my relationship with Rand with him. I dig into my five-cheese ziti like it's the first meal I've eaten in a month. Koop cuts his veal parmesan into delicate bites before popping them one by one into his mouth. It's fairly obvious that he was raised attending important dinner parties and social events. I suddenly feel like an undignified slob. I put my fork down and dab at the corners of my mouth with the cloth napkin.

"What do you love about Mitzi?" I ask, sipping my ice water.

"She was pretty, smart, athletic. Just the whole package," he answers.

"When is the last time you saw her?" I figure we've had enough small talk and it's time to get down to business.

"The night before she disappeared she came to my room," Koop says vaguely, with a faraway look in his eyes. "She wanted out of the Zeta house. I think she told them and they killed her," he says matter-of-factly, popping another bite into his mouth.

"Just for wanting out of the sorority? That seems a little harsh." The sisters were weird but I had yet to see anyone display hardcore rage issues.

"Can we talk about something else, please?" he asks, pouring himself a second glass of wine.

"Sure, sorry. I was just hoping to get some information that would help me find her for you," I tell him.

"Yeah, it would be nice to have some closure." I realize that he's given up thinking that she is alive. He just wants to know what happened to her once and for all. I guess I can't blame him. Harry always told me if the victim isn't found within forty-eight hours, all bets are usually off. He was amazed that Lulu hadn't offed Angel. Poor Mitzi's been gone for a few months now. The more I think about it, I have to admit it is a little crazy to think she is still alive somewhere, especially after she lost all that blood.

"You must live a pretty cush life, Koop," I say, switching the conversation to his family's wealth.

"I can't complain. Dad keeps me on a short leash though. I just found out today that I'm being forced to spend my Christmas vacation in Belize. No one even asks me where I want to go," he whines, sounding like a spoiled toddler.

"Oh, poor little trust-fund baby!" I say, making fun of him.

"Yeah, I guess it probably does sound pretty lame." He laughs. He reaches across the table and takes my hand. I sit there stunned not knowing what to do.

"I'm so glad you are here with me, Aspen. It's been so hard the last few months. Thank you for helping me," he says, then kisses the top of my hand. I'm about to yank it away when I hear yelling.

"What the hell is this?" Rand demands, standing red faced beside our table.

"Dude, chill. We're just having dinner," Koop says, trying to calm Rand down. I yank my hand away and get up to hug Rand.

"Listen, I only came here because he sent me a text from your phone," I say, busting Koop out. I'm not about to let Rand think I'm going behind his back to have a secret rendezvous with Koop.

"Aspen, wake up. He's trying to come between us," Rand slurs.

"Are you drunk again?" I yell. "I thought you were supposed to be studying."

"We just had a few beers with our big brothers. I wasn't out on some date behind your back."

"Rand Bachrach, you better take that back," I demand.

"Whatever," he says, untangling himself from me and

slouching down into my chair. "You'd probably be better off with him anyway. I always knew I'd lose you eventually," Rand says, getting weepy.

"God, I hate people who can't handle their booze," Koop says, taking a swig of wine.

"Shut up and help me get him out of here."

Koop throws down a fifty for our bill, then we maneuver Rand between us against his many protests. We finally get him into Koop's car where he is unconscious for most of the ride back to the dorm. I look down at my outfit in despair. What a waste of designer duds. Rand didn't even notice that I'd dressed up for him tonight. In his defense, I guess he probably thought I was dressed up for Koop. Part of me wonders if maybe Rand is right. Could Koop be playing some sick game to try and come between us? Nah, I don't think even he could be that twisted. To use his missing ex-girlfriend to try and get close to me, it was too horrible to even contemplate.

"I hope that Rand isn't right," I say to Koop, pulling down the visor mirror.

"What are you talking about?" he asks innocently.

"I hope you aren't trying to come between us. Very bad things happen to people who try to come between Rand and me," I say cryptically, reapplying my lip gloss, thinking of Amy. Amy tried desperately to sway Rand out of love with me last year. She ended up being one of Lulu's kidnapping victims and last I heard, she was the bikini girl at the local carwash. Detailing the cars of dirty old men in a skimpy bikini for minimum wage. It gives me shivers just thinking about it.

"I'll consider myself warned," Koop says with a smirk.

Between the two of us we finally manage to get Rand back to his dorm room. Koop promises to look after him, which I don't believe for a second, but I'm not up for spending another night worrying that Rand will wake up and throw up in my hair. I bend down to kiss him on the cheek before I leave even though I'm kind of pissed at him. This drunk routine is getting old. He stirs as my lips touch his cheek and his eyes open wide.

"I'm sorry for acting like a jerk. I went to your room and all your stuff was gone. I got scared," he says, and then passes out again.

I hadn't even considered that Rand had gone to my room and saw it empty. I hadn't had a chance to tell him about the move. No wonder he acted so crazy at the restaurant. I bend down and kiss him again feeling guilty for worrying him. I'd explain it all to him tomorrow when he was sober. Koop disappeared into the bathroom and I have a feeling the bottle of red he put away wasn't settling with him so well. It serves him right for all those cracks he made about Rand at the restaurant. I wonder if Mitzi really loved Koop and if so, why? He's hotter than a firecracker but his personality sucks. Is it possible that she really saw something special in him? Nah, she was probably just with him for his money.

I head upstairs to change out of Angel's dress. As I slip

out of it and back into the sweat clothes, I wonder if my body will reject them after being in such a luxurious garment all night. I can hardly wait until Cassandra deems me worthy enough to wear civilian clothes again.

I putter around Angel's room for a bit, not looking forward to unpacking all my stuff again at the Zeta house. I'm so tired that I just want to sleep, but Angel might find it a little odd if she comes home to find me passed out in her bed.

I rehang Angel's dress with care and put her shoes back into their designated box. I leave a little note thanking her. Sometimes I still can't get over the fact that just a year ago we were archenemies, and now as I glance around my empty side of the room, I feel a little depressed. This will probably be the last time that I'm here alone. Angel will get a new roomie and be so busy having fun with the Betas that she might just forget all about me. Okay, I know that wouldn't happen, who could forget about me? But we'll drift apart, that I know for sure.

Loud banging comes from the door interrupting my moment. Had Rand woken up already? Were the Zetas hunting me down? Was Rand right and Koop was waiting outside the door ready to ravish my sweat-clothed body? I eased the door open gently, not prepared at all for who I saw.

"Where is she, Aspen?" my ex- and Angel's current boyfriend, Lucas, demands. He practically steamrolls me to get inside our dorm room. I close the door behind him still in shock.

"Lucas, what are you doing here?" I ask, taking in his still shaggy blond hair, noticeably bigger pecs, and still amazing quarterback butt. He is a sight for my sore eyes.

"She moved out?" he asks, his voice raising an octave, as he takes in my empty side of the room. "Where did she go? I've got to find her. Did she get kidnapped like that other girl?" he says, out of control with panic, pacing the room.

"Lucas, relax. She didn't move out. I did. I'm moving to the sorority house. Angel is just out with her sisters tonight," I tell him, putting a hand on his shoulder.

"I've got to see her, Aspen. Something's going on. She won't return my calls. Is she with some other dude? Are you covering up for her? I can't lose her, Aspen. She's everything to me," he pleads.

"Come on," I say, linking my arm through his. I lead him down the stairs to the elevator and we start our trek to Greek Row.

"No offense, Aspen, but you're kind of letting yourself go," Lucas says, looking down at my clothes.

"The Zetas are making me wear these," I explain, feeling like a frumpy housewife.

"I didn't think anybody could make you do anything." He laughs, poking me in the ribs.

"It's complicated. Let's just say that when I get what I

want, I'm outta there," I verbalize for the first time. The closer we get to Greek Row the more uncomfortable I am. Even with Lucas by my side, I feel unsafe somehow. A twig snaps behind us and we both spin around but can't see anything on the pitch-dark quad.

"It's really sweet that you came all the way here. Angel is really lucky." I punch him in the arm playfully. Lucas and I always worked better in a brother/sister relationship than as a couple. It feels good to have a little piece of home around even if it's only for a few minutes.

"What if she's with some other dude?" Lucas asks nervously, as we approach the front door of the Beta house.

"You're her only dude, Lucas. I promise. Her parents' divorce got her all jacked up and she's got some trust issues. Just be patient with her."

We hear howls of laughter coming from the house. It sounds like I always thought a sorority house should sound.

"Do you think they are having pillow fights in just their panties?" Lucas asks, excited.

"I'm sure that's exactly what they're doing, Lucas." I laugh, banging on the door.

The door flings open and I recognize the girl who escorted me inside the night of the recruitment party.

"Hi, Aspen," she says, brightly. She takes in Lucas appreciatively.

"Is Angel here? This is her boyfriend . . ." I start to introduce Lucas but her screams cut me off.

"Oh my God, you're Lucas," she says, jumping up and down.

"Yeah, I am." Lucas blushes.

"She's gonna freak." She grabs a few sisters who are walking by with a pizza and tells them to get Angel but not to tell her why.

A few seconds later, Angel comes bounding down a flight of stairs looking incredible. Her makeup is done perfectly showing no signs of excess like usual. Her short black hair is rolled into shiny fat curls all over her head. She is wearing a tiny pink slip dress that clings to her as she comes down the stairs. I've never seen her look so incredible.

Lucas sees her way before she sees him and he is speechless. She finally looks directly at him, then at me, but it doesn't seem to register. Lucas doesn't wait for her to say anything but just leaps across the threshold, scoops her up, and starts kissing her long and hard. She wraps her black manicured nails around his head and pulls him more deeply into the kiss. Her sisters all scream and clap with joy for her. They must have known that she was having a hard time and contemplating breaking up with Lucas. I can tell by Angel's attitude and attire that the Betas have had a positive influence on her. Angel is lucky to have Lucas and the sisters, and they are lucky to have her.

My work here is so done. I slink back to the Zeta house ready to drop from exhaustion.

The Zeta house is pitch black and while I'm overjoyed that I won't have to deal with anybody tonight, I have no clue where my stuff is. I open the unlocked front door (Harry would have a field day with that) and sneak quietly into the foyer. I slip off my tennis shoes so that they don't squeak. I've already decided to spend the night on one of the couches in the great room so that I don't wake anyone up.

Suddenly the room is as bright as daylight and all the sisters are sitting on the stairs in their pajamas giving me dirty looks. Cassandra stands at the top of the stairs wearing Zeta boxer shorts and a tank top with her hands on her hips.

"Do you have any idea how worried we've been?" she asks, glaring at me.

"Oh, sorry. I had some stuff to take care of. You didn't have to wait up," I answer, taken back. My *parents* have never interrogated me like this so I'm not really sure how I'm supposed to react to the Zeta firing squad.

"Of course we did. You didn't have your keys," she says, tossing me a key ring jammed with keys.

"What are the rest of these for?" I ask, twirling the keys around my finger.

"For the door, duh," Grey smarts off. "I'm going to go check the perimeter. I'll be back," she says, disappearing out the door. The little bit I've been around Grey she seems a little scary. Not to mention that she acts like she is Cassandra's personal bodyguard.

I start to laugh then realize I'm the only one laughing. I try my best to cork it up but a few giggles escape. I glance toward the back of the door and see they weren't lying. The door has about ten deadbolts on it. I toss the keys up in the air and catch them. I'm going to look like my old high school janitor carrying all these freaking keys around.

Grey busts through the door then bolts all the locks with record speed. She is dressed all in black with two smears of black shoe polish under her eyes.

"The perimeter is secure," Grey reports to Cassandra. I bury my mouth in my arm and fake cough to keep from busting a gut laughing.

"What kind of stuff were you up to tonight?" she asks, and all the sisters seem to raise their eyebrows suspiciously at the same time.

"Studying?" I answer, but it comes out sounding more like a question. I am so glad that I changed clothes at the dorm. I can't imagine the treatment I'd be getting if I was standing here in a Betsey Johnson dress.

"Where are your books?" Cassandra asks, totally on to me. I want to tell her to stick it where the sun don't shine and run screaming from the house but I know that I can't. Not yet anyway. I have to play along until I get the information that I need. A good mole never backs down in the face of a little adversity.

"Aspen says she was studying all night, Grey. Can you confirm that?" Cassandra asks her.

What? The Zetas are having me tailed? These beyotches are crazier than I thought. I try to run through the evening in my head to figure out what Grey could have seen.

"Not unless she's studying anatomy." Grey laughs, pulling a hand towel from one of the pockets in her utility pants, wiping her face.

"English please, Grey," Cassandra says, getting annoyed.

"Our new member likes to get around with members of the opposite sex. Tonight alone I saw her with some old guy, a total hottie, some drunk guy, and a surfer dude."

I thought about how the night had unfolded starting with Harry, dinner with Koop that was busted up by Rand, then the entertainment portion of the evening provided by Lucas. I couldn't help but smile at how it must have looked to an outsider.

"Is that true, Aspen? Are you easy?" Cassandra asks.

"I'm going to pretend that you didn't just ask me that," I say, giving her a warning look.

"If you want to be a slut, you should join the Betas," she says, and all the girls nod in agreement.

My face practically bursts into flames I'm so pissed. How dare she talk about the Betas that way. I want to tell her off so bad but I know that would be disastrous. I ball up my fists at my sides and try to get control of myself before I speak.

"I appreciate that you have a reputation to uphold and I can assure you, I'm not spreading myself around." I see Charm peeking out from behind a blonde giving me a thumbs-up. I take it to mean that I am doing a good job standing my own with Cassandra.

"She went to the Beta house tonight wearing civilian clothes," Grey says, which causes all the sisters to shriek.

"Zetas do not socialize with Betas. Ever! Do you understand?" Cassandra scolds me.

I nod while trying to figure out how I am going to skulk around being friends with Angel without the Zetas knowing, and without Angel knowing I'm not supposed to be friends with her. I was exhausted just thinking about it. At least no one seemed to hear Grey bust me out for ditching my sweats!

"We need more focus from you, Aspen. If you want to be a Zeta, you have to live the Zeta life. We have rules and expectations. Tomorrow is a new day; we'll discuss it all then. You got some dirt on the floor. Get a towel and wipe it up. Time for bed girls," she says, disappearing down the hall with a line of girls following behind her going to their rooms. Charm stays behind waiting for me.

"That was awesome. You really gave it back to her. Nobody ever talks to Cassandra like that," Charm says, pumped up.

"I would have liked to tell her a lot more than that, believe me," I say, stripping off my Zeta sweatshirt and using it to clean up the floor.

"I thought you were going to burst into flames when she called you easy," she says, laughing.

"I've been called worse by better," I reply. Thinking about it starts getting me upset again. I know that I will have to stay as far away from Cassandra as possible if I am going to make it in this house. After I have what I need or Tobi is okay, whichever is first, then I might just hunt down Cassandra in a dark alley some night.

"So do you know where I'm bunking?" I ask, more than ready for bed.

"Yeah, with me," Charm says excitedly. It was the best news I'd had all day. Something was finally going my way. I didn't even let the creepy thought that I would be occupying Mitzi's old spot ruin it for me. Who knows, maybe she had left something behind that I would find.

We disappear up the stairs laughing, getting hushed by the sisters as we sneak by their rooms. We get to our room and Charm stands nervously at the door. Slowly she turns the knob and I can see that all of my things have been unpacked and put away with loving care. Even my familiar bedding is draped over the bed across from Charm's. I have to admit that no matter how annoying the Zetas could be, this house is the bomb. I fling open the closet door to find all my clothes hung and in pristine condition. My textbooks are stacked neatly on my desk alongside my laptop.

"I hope it's okay that I unpacked for you," Charm says nervously.

"It's more than okay. Everything looks great, really great," I tell her flopping onto my bed. I don't even bother changing my clothes, I just slip under the covers.

She flings her backpack onto her bed and for a minute I think the weight might collapse it. She flips on a little reading lamp.

"Will it bother you if I study?" she asks, cracking open a textbook.

"I don't think it would bother me if you drove a Mac truck through the room," I tell her, my eyes getting heavy. I hear her laugh for a second then pure silence.

My phone beeps in my purse next to my bed. I pick it up and retrieve a text message.

100x better lk club med 4 sick ppl here how do u do it luv u Tobi

I slip my phone back into my purse while smiling to myself. I feel much better knowing that all this torture is for a good cause. I drift away dreaming of Rand and me sunning ourselves on an exotic beach.

A few second later, a horrible screeching noise comes from the ceiling. I bolt up in bed.

"What the hell was that?"

"Our room is directly under the attic. The squirrels get up there at night and go crazy," Charm says, looking up nervously.

"Can't anybody go up there and do something?" I ask.

"They're rabid. It's best just to leave them alone," she suggests. I remember the look the squirrel on campus gave me after I impaled his tail and know that there is no way I'll be going up there.

I fall asleep and dream about Cassandra contracting rabies and foaming from the mouth. It's a good dream.

Nine

So I wake up and totally don't know where I'm at, then I hear those damn squirrels fornicating above me and it all comes flooding back. What a night! I sit up to get out of bed and Charm is in the exact same position I left her when I went to bed.

"Have you even slept?" I ask her, stretching my arms to the ceiling. My new mattress was ten times more comfortable than the one at the concrete jungle. I just hope they replaced it because that would be super foul to be sleeping on the bed that had all of Mitzi's blood on it. It makes me shiver just thinking about it.

"Yeah, I got about three hours in," Charm says, distracted. Three hours of sleep, her hair is pulled into a bun with a number two pencil, and the girl still looks amazing.

"I've never met anyone like you before," I tell her, grabbing some clean clothes to change into after showering.

"What do you mean?" she asks, finally looking up from her book.

"You're a real perfectionist. We're a lot alike," I confess.

"It can be a curse sometimes," she says, suddenly looking exhausted.

"But it's always worth it in the end," I remind her. It was like me with my investigation. There was nothing I wanted less than a bunch of pathetic girls who have to pay for their friends to boss me around, but when I start something, I'm in it for the long haul. Which reminds me that I really need to get busy snooping around the house today for clues. I have no idea what I'm looking for; I just hope I can find something and I need to start right away.

"Is there a bathroom around here somewhere?" I ask, hoping that it is better than the one at the dorm.

Charm's head is already buried deep in her book again but she lifts an arm and points to a door that I thought was an extra closet.

"We have our own bathroom?" I squeal. She nods. Okay, I can take a hint; the girl's a bookworm. At least I won't have to worry about her wanting to chat me up all the time. Because I've got plenty of stuff to do and I don't need to be babysitting some girl who wants to bond.

I spend at least an hour in the bathroom. I hope that I managed to completely drain the hot water heater and that Cassandra hasn't taken her shower yet. It would serve her right for calling me easy. Charm is gone by the time I get out. She left a note saying she would be at the library all day.

I slip into my favorite purple and gray argyle sweater and jeans. I'm finishing my outfit off with the diamond studs that Rand gave me when I drop one into the carpet. Panic seizes me and I drop to the floor to look for it. I run my hands over the carpet feeling for it. After five minutes with no luck I fan my search out over more square footage. I run my hands slowly over the carpet hoping to feel it, but I don't. The sunlight glittering through the window catches on something near the baseboard. I crawl over but don't see anything. I put my hand down against the edge of the carpet and the baseboard and feel something metal. It's wedged under the fabric. I yank the edge of the carpet up a tiny bit and pull out a gold locket. It looks a lot like one I had in middle school. The locket is in the shape of a heart and engraved with the initial *M*.

Could it be my first actual clue? I pop the locket open to find a heart-shaped picture of a miniature Mitzi and Cassandra. That's strange, why would Mitzi want to wear a picture of Cassandra around her neck? I snap it shut and flip the heart over to see a tiny speck of blood. The delicate chain that holds the locket is broken. I almost drop the necklace as I realize that this was probably pulled off Mitzi's neck during the struggle. I close my hand around the necklace just as the door to my room opens.

"Why are you wearing those clothes?" Cassandra asks, barging into the room.

"I figured I'd be here all day so I didn't think it would matter what I wore," I bluff.

"Oh, I guess that's okay. We're all having breakfast and I'd really like you to join us," she says, semipleasantly.

"I'll be there in just a second," I tell her, knowing I'm not leaving the room until I find my other earring.

"I'd really like it if you came right now," Cassandra says, on her power trip again. She starts walking back to the door when she yelps in pain. "What the heck?" She looks down at her heel to see my earring sticking out of it. I run over and pull it out, deliriously happy that it was found.

"Thanks, Cassandra, I thought I'd lost that," I tell her then run to the bathroom to disinfect it before putting it in my ear. I hear her huff out of the room as I delicately drop the locket into my makeup bag.

⊙

Minutes later I'm enjoying a scrumptious breakfast of bacon, eggs, and sausage crowded around a tiny table in the kitchen. I contemplate asking why we aren't using the gigantic dining room, but then I recall Cassandra's borderline obsession with cleanliness. I'm sure she doesn't want to soil the beautiful linens and china. Everyone is being very nice and I'm almost fooled into thinking they are more than Zeta robots. Grey hands me a glass of water, which I accept without making eye contact. I know after last night that she isn't to be trusted and from now on I'll definitely be watching my back.

"Can I get some toast?" I ask no one in particular. Gasps go up throughout the room as if I just asked for some crack or something. "Don't we have a cook?" I ask, eye-balling Grey near the stove. I wouldn't put it past her to poison me. Maybe she did something to Mitzi.

"Girls, it's okay. Poor Aspen isn't even familiar with our special diet yet," Cassandra says from the head of the table. I watch as all of the girls rest their forks on their plates and even stop chewing in anticipation of Cassandra's next words.

"Zeta girls don't eat carbs," she explains. "We know how important it is to keep a good figure and carbs just don't agree with our bodies." She nibbles on a piece of bacon while I contemplate this.

"So you don't eat any fruit or bread or sweets at all?" I ask, clarifying.

"That's right," she says, stabbing a sausage patty with her fork. "And I fired the cook because she kept trying to sneak in fruits and vegetables."

"Doesn't eating meat all the time give you high cholesterol?" I ask, pointing out the obvious. After all, didn't that Atkins guy die of a heart attack? Eating a pound of bacon, butter, cheese, and eggs a day doesn't sound like the healthiest diet in the world.

"We're young, we don't have to worry about our cholesterol until we're at least in our fifties," she says matter-of-factly.

I contemplate telling her that I have low blood sugar so I have to have some juice and sweets, but then I see her looking over at me like she's reading my mind. I guess a little red meat never hurt anyone.

"If it will give me thighs like yours, I guess I'm up for it." I laugh. She looks at me, surprised, like she doesn't know how to take my compliment, and then she smiles. She would be almost pretty when she smiles if it weren't for those huge eyes and lips.

"What are the other rules?" I ask, ready to get it all out in the open.

"Every sister must keep at least a three point zero grade point average every semester plus volunteer with a local charity. You can only leave campus twice a semester to go home, and absolutely no boys in the house," Cassandra finishes, looking pleased. The other sisters still aren't eating and their eyes are going back and forth between Cassandra and me like they are watching a tennis match.

"My boyfriend is a Nu; is that acceptable?" I ask, knowing I'm going to tell her to kiss it if it's not.

"What do you mean?" she asks, confused.

"I thought maybe you required the girls to date guys out of a specific fraternity," I say.

"I don't really care who you date as long as it doesn't interfere with your life in the Zeta house."

"So you're saying that if I wanted to date a GDI, I could?"

"Aspen, that's such an outdated term, but yes, if you wanted to date someone outside of Greek Row that's none of our business. I would never tell someone who to fall in love with," she says wistfully.

Why would Mitzi lie to Koop? If Cassandra really didn't care who the Zetas date, what other reason would Mitzi have to hide Koop away? I have to find out.

"If that's all, I have some errands to run," Cassandra says, getting up from the table and leaving the room. Grey takes Cassandra's plate and puts it in the sink. The girls immediately start chatting and eating again.

"Who was the old dude you were with last night?" A girl named Lucy leans over and asks me. She was really sweet on rush night and even asked to see a picture of my parents.

"Just some guy I asked for a ride across campus," I say, knowing it will shock the crap out of her. I'm positive that hitchhiking is right up there on the list of Zeta no-nos with bread and apples.

"That's cool. I like older men," she says dreamily. A piece of bacon flies through the air and pegs her in the forehead. "Hey," she says, glaring at Mary-Margaret, my escort from rush night, who threw it at her. "What the hell?"

"You're such a bitch. I hate you," Mary-Margaret spits out then reaches across all the breakfast meat and grabs Lucy. They proceed to bitch slap each other for several minutes and it takes all the sisters, with the exception of me, Jocelyn, and Lilly, to get them under control. I sit quietly munching my bacon watching the whole scene unfold while Lilly is asleep with her head on top of her folded arms on the table. Jocelyn doesn't take her thumb out of her mouth for anything. My dad's favorite phrase, "This is better than TV," comes to mind.

"Lucy, Mary-Margaret, you guys cool down. Just go upstairs and stay away from each other," Grey says, taking command in Cassandra's absence.

The girl's scoot their chairs back and leave the room one at a time.

"I thought that was all settled," Grey says, shaking her head.

"How settled do you think you'd be if somebody seduced your dad on Parents' Weekend?" a petite redhead says. I nearly choke on my bacon remembering Lucy's comment about how cute my dad is. Gross!

"Lucy slept with Mary-Margaret's dad?" I ask, hoping I'm misunderstanding. All the sisters nod their heads yes. "Oh my God, that's so messed up." I laugh, getting a dirty look from Grey. I didn't blame Mary-Margaret at all for going after Lucy, but I was glad that I knew to watch out for my own dad and Harry around Lucy.

"What are you doing today, Aspen?" Grey asks. I'm

sure she isn't really curious but just wants to plan her day around stalking me.

"I've barely studied since I got here. I'll be in my room hitting the books all day," I answer honestly. Luckily, last week most of my professors just went over their syllabuses. Which normally is beyond annoying, I mean, I can read. But since I haven't exactly been academically focused since I got here, it was a relief!

"Sounds like a plan. It shouldn't take you long to do the dishes since not everyone was here for breakfast. Cassandra likes them triple-washed and towel dried. There should be absolutely no water spots or film on them," she orders like a militant Martha Stewart, pushing her chair away from the table. I can't even try to hide the shock I'm feeling. Me? Do dishes? With no dishwasher? I look to the stove, overflowing with pans filled with grease, and want to cry. I wish my mom were here. She'd clean up everything and never expect me to help. I force a smile while gathering plates as the sisters pile happily out of the kitchen.

As if doing dishes isn't bad enough, they didn't even give me any gloves. So now my hands are wrinkled like prunes and I can't stand touching paper when my hands are like that so that means I can't study right now. I go back to my room and hunt down my cell phone. I find it in my purse and I already have five messages. I quickly go through them, one from Tobi who is sounding very chipper, three from Rand sounding increasingly desperate, and one from Koop. I dial Rand first.

"Where are you?" he answers desperately.

"Rand, calm down. I live at the Zeta house now. They moved my stuff over here yesterday. You were so drunk last night I didn't have a chance to tell you," I explain.

"Why were you with him?" he whispers, telling me that Koop must be there with him.

"I told you. He texted me on your phone. I thought I was meeting you. I only stayed because I thought he might tell me something about Mitzi that would help move this thing along a little."

"And?"

"Then you busted in and nearly got us kicked out of the restaurant. I don't think he knows anything anyway. I found my first clue today," I whisper with excitement.

"What was it?"

"Mitzi's locket, it's even got blood on it." I know I shouldn't be excited about finding a missing girl's jewelry but I can't help it.

"Where did you find that?" he asks, disgusted.

"On the floor in my room. It was stuck under the edge of the carpeting." I still couldn't believe how lucky I'd gotten by dropping that earring. I'd found something that even the campus police hadn't found, although Harry keeps saying they couldn't tell their asses from a hole in the ground so maybe I shouldn't get so excited.

"Are you staying in the same room that she lived in?" Rand asks, creeped out.

"Yeah, so?"

"Isn't that kind of weird?"

Well, it wasn't until he pointed it out. Now I'm looking around the room with different eyes. What if Mitzi is dead but she's haunting the Zeta house? What if those aren't really squirrels in the attic but the ghost of Mitzi?

"Aspen?" Rand asks, and I shriek.

"Why did you have to go and get me all freaked out?"

"Do you want me to come over there and keep you company?" he offers seductively.

"That's very tempting but there are no boys allowed at the Zeta house. The Zetas take their reputations very seriously," I say, doing my best Cassandra impression.

"That blows. I need to study anyway."

"Yeah, me too. With everything else that's been going on, our education, the whole reason why we are here, kind of got blown off." I laugh.

"Are you actually supposed to learn stuff in college?" He laughs too.

"Not if you keep getting blitzed every night," I say, wanting to send him a message without lecturing him.

"I know, I'm sorry about that. The guys are just so much fun, it's hard to say no to them." I understand completely and I know we will both get back on track soon.

"Hey, I've got to call Koop but I want to put you on the other line so you know exactly how long I talk to him. So pretend like we are saying good-bye but don't hang up," I say, knowing that Koop would do just about anything to get under Rand's skin. I click over to a new line and dial Koop's number.

"Koop, do you remember if Mitzi ever wore anything all the time, like jewelry or anything?" I ask as soon as he answers. I wanted confirmation that the necklace was hers, even though I knew it was, but I really wanted to know if it was something she just wore part of the time or if it was sort of her trademark.

"Hey, Aspen," he practically shouts for Rand's benefit. I hold the phone away from my ear and roll my eyes.

"Answer the question, Koop," I say, getting irritated with him.

"Hmmm . . . nothing really stands out, but she didn't really wear a whole lot of anything when we were together. If you know what I mean." He laughs, sounding like a greasy gigolo.

"That's all I wanted. Thanks," I say, clicking off before he can get another word out. I click back over to Rand.

"Is he still talking to me?" I ask Rand.

He's silent for a minute then starts cracking up. I hear him say, "Dude, I know you aren't talking to her anymore because I am." He gets back on the phone, his mood much improved.

"No one is ever going to come between us, not some fraternity full of drunk guys or some trust-fund player, okay?" I say, hoping I've eased his mind a little.

"You're the best girlfriend ever," he says, and I can hear his enormous smile.

"Tell me something I don't know," I say, clicking off.

@

Studying gets old really fast, besides I read somewhere that you should take lots of breaks while studying so your brain can rest or something. I walk to the kitchen to let my brain rest, hoping to sneak a snack.

"Where are you going?" Cassandra asks, sneaking up behind me like a ninja.

"Jesus, Cassandra, relax. I just wanted a snack," I say, putting my hand over my racing heart.

"There is a bowl of beef jerky in the great room," she says. Yum, beef jerky, not! I notice that she is carrying two large leather-bound photo albums.

"What are those?"

"Just some pictures of the sisters from the last few years." She shrugs.

"Oh, can I see them?" I ask, excitedly. She brightens, thinking I'm actually interested in all these crazy drones she calls sisters, when really I just want to see pictures of Mitzi and whether she's wearing the necklace.

"Of course," she says, walking into a parlor area and taking a seat on a velvet sofa. She obviously isn't going to hand over the books so I guess I'll be spending some quality time with her.

After twenty minutes of sheer boredom, I'm ready to jump out a window. How many pictures of girls in Zeta sweatshirts is a girl supposed to look at? Then the same picture from Mitzi's locket jumps off the pages of the photo album at me. I point to it and wait to see what Cassandra says. She doesn't say anything just flips to the next page, which is filled with pictures of Mitzi. She is wearing the locket in every single one of them. I knew it. She wouldn't have lost that necklace without a serious fight.

"That's Mitzi, isn't it?" I ask innocently since I'm not really supposed to know anything about her.

"Yes, that's Mitzi." She sighs.

"She's really pretty and I love that locket she's wearing," I probe.

"I gave that to her. We were really close," she says sadly, her thoughts drifting. "She was my little sister," she explains, pulling back into the present. That would explain why Mitzi would wear a picture of them together. I wonder why I haven't gotten a big sister yet.

"What do you think happened?" I ask, hoping I don't scare her off.

"Whatever happened here was bad. No one can lose that much blood and still be alive. But it doesn't make any sense. She didn't have any enemies," she says, slamming the photo album shut. "It's really hard for the girls to talk about her, so it would be best if you didn't," Cassandra warns. I nod my head, realizing for the first time that I wasn't investigating a missing person's case. I was investigating a murder.

◎

"I can't believe they let you out of their sight for more than five minutes," Angel smarts off, handing me a cup of hot chocolate as I sit down next to her in Abnormal Psych the next day.

"And here I thought you'd be in such a great mood because I got you laid Saturday night," I tease her. Her eyes go dreamy and I know she's remembering Lucas picking her up and kissing her. "I never thought in a million years that I'd be saying this, but you guys make a great couple," I tell her.

"We do, don't we?" she agrees.

"So I take it everything's kosher now?" I really hope so because I was beginning to fear for my cell phone battery as many times as Lucas was calling me to try to find Angel.

"Yeah, we're cool. So did my dress end up on Rand's floor the other night or what?" she asks, taking a sip of her coffee.

"Not hardly. First, Harry nearly gives me a heart attack stalking me on campus, and then dinner was a total fiasco. It turns out that Koop was the one who asked me to dinner, not Rand, then Rand busts in on us, totally plastered, thinking we are getting it on behind his back, then Koop and I had to get Rand back to the dorm, and that's about the time that Lucas nearly beat our door down. After that I was met at the front door by the Zeta firing squad for being out so late. So, yeah, you could say that my weekend had all the makings of a really bad B movie. Oh, yeah, and I can't have carbs anymore," I say, handing the hot chocolate back to her as I spot Grey, dressed all in black and hidden like a sniper, in the back row of the auditorium. I do a quick up-down of Angel to make sure she isn't wearing her letters or anything that would give her away as a Beta. Thankfully she isn't so I won't have to get up and walk away from her. I'm sure I only have a few days before Grey finds out Angel's affiliation with the Betas though.

It's not until I see Angel's mouth hanging open that I realize I just said all of that out loud. Oops. It just feels so good to have a friend to talk to that I didn't realize I was spouting off about things that really should have been kept secret. Nice undercover work.

"Who's Koop? And why was Harry here?" Angel asks, cocking her head to the side in confusion.

Fabulous. I know there is no way I can bluff Angel; she knows me too well. I choose my words very carefully.

"Koop is Rand's roommate. He's kind of repulsive in a completely godlike hot way. You'd love him. And Harry was just in the neighborhood to lecture me about campus security," I explain. Her eyes narrow in on me and I try to stay calm. It wasn't really a lie; I have nothing to be pan-icked about. I force a smile and break out my notebook ready to take notes.

"Does he like you or something?"

"Oh, yeah, we've been real close since the Lulu thing went down," I say, knowing full well she's talking about Koop and not Harry.

She gives me a dirty look. I shrug innocently and act clueless.

"I meant Koop. Does Koop like you? I mean, he must if he's trying to get you to dinner."

"Oh, who knows? He's one of those guys who only wants what he can't have. He just knows I'm unattainable and can't help himself," I say conceitedly. Angel rolls her eyes and gets out her notebook.

"Get over yourself," she whispers as Professor Brown taps his microphone and starts the lecture.

I'm relieved and sad all at the same time. Relieved that Angel won't be sneaking around trying to figure out what I'm up to, but sad that I can't tell one of my only true friends here what is really going on with me.

I try to focus on what Professor Brown is saying but my mind isn't cooperating. Then he flashes a picture of a guy who is semihot, in a totally outdated seventies side-burns kind of way, on the overhead projector. He asks how many women in the class think he's nice looking. Now this is a lecture I can get into. Tons of whoops and hollers go up, and then he sets another picture alongside it of a sorority house. He explains that this hottie, Ted Bundy, broke into a Florida sorority house one night and killed two women and critically injured two more. Those were just a few of his victims. They only know for sure of thirty women he killed but think there are lots more. He was a completely functioning member of society but a serial killer to the core. Yikes! Note to self: Never talk to strange men even if they are wearing a full body cast. I wonder for a second if Ted could have come and taken Mitzi. I mean, he obviously has a thing for sorority babes. Then Professor Brown explains that Ted had been fried clear back in 1989, a few months before I was even born. So much for that theory.

Ten

The next few weeks are a blur of tests. I ace every single one of them, even in chem, which I despise with a passion normally reserved for fake designer purses. It is turning colder outside already, and some days, I am actually thankful for the warmth of my hideous Zeta sweats. Koop has taken to texting me or calling me at least twice a day, which is beyond annoying, but I don't want to blow him off because Tobi is doing a million times better and she only has a few weeks of observation left. I know that once she can prove to the doctors she is better there is nothing Koop can do. His dad wouldn't trade all the free publicity for his new drug for the world, even if his son was unhappy.

Koop never wants anything specific. It is always little

tidbits like "I just remembered that Mitzi's favorite color was green." Like, oh yeah, that's gonna break the case wide open. I have a feeling he's just lonely. All his money and looks haven't been able to get him any true friends.

Rand spends almost all of his time at the Nu house just to avoid him. And even though the Nus share a backyard with us, I barely see him. I love that he's found a new group of friends, but I'm not exactly hot on just being a side dish these days. I plan to rectify that situation as soon as I get out of the Zeta house.

I haven't been able to get much out of the sisters about Mitzi. Charm spends every waking second in the library studying. I completely understand now how she didn't really know much about Mitzi. Most of the time I feel like I'm living alone.

But it is like that with all of the girls. They all live together in a gorgeous mansion but they don't bond like girlfriends do. We spend a lot of time talking about the weather and our classes, but nothing of any real importance. I know that trying to find out anything about Mitzi from these girls is a lost cause.

"Hey, Charm? Is there anywhere besides the attic that we can store stuff? I kind of want to put away my summer clothes," I ask her, getting an idea.

"Oh, sure. We've got a basement. You can put your stuff down there. It's off the kitchen," she says, heading out the door looking like a hunchback from the weight of her backpack.

"Great, thanks." I wave good-bye to her, then run to our window and watch all of sisters leave for classes. Lilly is the only one I can't account for but I know she's passed out somewhere so I'm not worried.

I walk through the deserted house into the kitchen and immediately find the door to the basement. I can't believe I didn't notice it before now. I turn the knob and the door creaks open. A mildew smell hits me immediately. I can already tell I'm going to have to take another shower after this little excursion. I creep down the stairs and they groan under my feet. I make it to the bottom and bat around for a cord to turn the light on. I finally find it and tug, turning on one dingy forty-watt lightbulb.

Cardboard boxes are stacked everywhere and I don't see a single one labeled. Why do people have to be so freaking unorganized? I figure Mitzi's stuff couldn't have been down here long so I try to look for the box with the least amount of dust on it. I pull open the flaps of the first box to find it full of Zeta sweat clothes. They have enough to dress every person on campus. I'm extremely tempted to burn the entire box but realize I may not have much time so I pull open another box. This one is full of old textbooks. I decide to rethink my search. What if the person who put Mitzi's stuff down here didn't want people nosing through it? If that were the case then they would put the box more toward the back. I weave in between the boxes until I find one in the back that looks relatively clean. I pull open the flap and am face to face with Mitzi's huge smile.

It is a picture of her and Harry in a pink frame. He has his arm wrapped around her and they are sitting in front of a cake that reads, "Happy 40th Birthday, Harry!" on it. Part of me keeps forgetting that Mitzi is more than just a girl who disappeared but that she is someone Harry loves. I dig through the box with a fury, intent on finding another clue, but the box is filled with textbooks, folders, and just a few other pictures. They are mostly duplicates of the ones I'd seen of her and Cassandra in the photo album. I'm discouraged, and worse, I have cobwebs in my hair. I start stacking the books neatly back in the box when a note sticking out of one of them catches my eye. I grab it and crunch it into my palm while replacing the rest of Mitzi's things. It probably isn't anything, just an old assignment or something, so I'm not in a big hurry to read it. Which is a good thing because when I feel something crash down on my head and I fall over on the cold cement floor, I know I won't be reading anything for a while.

"Ew, that's gonna leave a mark," I say, touching the goose egg already forming on the top of my head. I'm lying on my back on a couch in the Zeta great room with all the sisters huddled around me.

"Back up girls, give her some air," Grey commands, and the sisters all take one step back. I try to sit up but the weight of my head pulls me back down. "Don't try to sit up," Grey says, pushing me back down gently. Is she actually being nice to me? Nah, it must be the head injury.

I close my eyes and take a few deep breaths, trying to remember what happened. I feel something clutched in my palm and remember finding the note then someone hitting me from behind. I have no doubt that someone hit me because there was nothing behind me that I could have bumped my head on, besides I never moved my head. No, someone had definitely whacked a home run on my skull. But why?

I was getting close and someone didn't like it.

"Who found me?" I ask, opening my eyes. Lucy holds her hand up halfway, smiling.

"At first I just thought you were sleeping," she says oblivious. "But I thought it was kind of weird you were asleep in the basement."

"Somebody get her some ice," Grey says, bossing the sisters around. "Hopefully we can get this swelling down. If we have to take her to the hospital, the Panhellenic council is going to revoke our charter for sure."

Gee, thanks for caring. I knew Grey being nice was too good to be true. I narrow my eyes at Grey wondering if she could be the one who knocked me out. She was supposed to be tailing me after all.

The front door opens and slams shut again, echoing through my head. A flustered Cassandra comes rushing over to me.

"Aspen, what happened? Did you fall down the

stairs?" she says, giving me the perfect excuse. I'm not about to freak all the sisters out by telling them that one of their own used my head for batting practice.

"I think I slipped on the last couple of steps. I was just trying to find a box for my summer clothes," I lie.

"I think we should take you to the hospital and get you checked out," she says, surprising me. Then I realize she doesn't give a crap if I'm okay. She just doesn't want another sister getting hurt or disappearing because she doesn't want to lose her charter. She is definitely not ruled out as a suspect.

"I'm fine," I lie, sitting up, careful to keep my hand closed to hide the note. "I just want to go lie down." A few sisters help me to my feet and take me to my room. I pop some aspirin to try to dull the throbbing pain in my head and crawl under my covers. There is no sign of Charm but it's already getting dark out so I know she'll be home soon. I must have been out for a long time. At least with all the sisters home I know I'll be safe. On second thought, I get up and lock the bedroom door.

Back in bed I unfold the note and do my best to read it even though my vision is a little blurry.

No one can ever find out about us.

I can tell that it is written in a girl's handwriting so Mitzi must have written it to someone but didn't have a chance to give it to them. Could this note have been meant for Koop? That didn't really make any sense though because he already knew she was keeping him a secret. Why write a note stating the obvious? Unless the note was for someone else. Could Mitzi have been having an affair behind Koop's back and this note was meant for her secret lover?

I am too tired to care right now. I drift to sleep even though I am pretty sure the squirrels in the attic are building a room addition.

I steer clear of Rand and Angel all the next day so that they won't see the tumor growing out of the back of my head. I try to cover it up with hats, but I just don't have the head to be a hat person, especially now.

Angel is in her own little Beta world so she is too busy to notice my absence. The Nus are having what Rand charmingly calls Hell Week so he isn't allowed to see or talk to me anyway so it works out well. I am afraid to ask what Hell Week consists of but I know he won't get himself in over his head. I, on the other hand, have my head to worry about so I focus on it.

The sisters are actually semidecent for a change. Charm fawns over me like I am dying and she even skips going to the library for a few hours to stay with me.

"You never talk about her," I say quietly, finally bringing up Mitzi, as we are watching television.

"It's just too hard," she answers not looking up.

"Was she dating anyone?"

Charm gets a funny look on her face but quickly composes herself. "No, I don't think so," she says.

"What was with the face?" I ask, tired of playing games.

"It's just that we never really talked about it, but I think maybe she was gay," she says, blushing.

Gay? Suddenly the note makes much more sense. Mitzi didn't write it—it was written for her. The locket flashes through my mind with the picture of Mitzi with Cassandra. Then I know. They weren't just sisters, they were lovers. Did Koop kill Mitzi in a jealous rage when he found out she was with Cassandra? Nah, he just would have wanted to watch. Did Cassandra kill Mitzi in a fit of passion when she found out about Koop? This scenario is much more likely. I've seen Cassandra in action and she can be one vicious bitch. I would bet money that she was the one who tried to off me in the basement. I know I can't do anything tonight but I have to call Harry the first chance I'm alone. He'll know what to do next.

"So I'm thinking that maybe Mitzi and Tobi might have some things in common," I whisper to Harry. I'm sneaking a call in while the other girls are eating dinner. I am excused from surf and turf night because of my "injury."

"Like what?" he asks, clueless.

I'm trying to be delicate telling him that Mitzi obviously likes girls and boys but he's not getting it and we are wasting precious phone time.

"Mitzi likes boys and girls," I finally say cringing. The line is silent for a few seconds. I so wish I wouldn't have had to tell him that.

"Harry? It's not that big of a deal. Look at Pippi and Tobi and they're full blown gay. Mitzi's only part gay," I say, trying to put a positive spin on it. I really didn't see why older people got so bent about sexual orientation. You love who you love, end of story.

"I always thought she was gay," he confesses. "That's why I was so confused when you said that she had a boyfriend. It just doesn't make any sense. How could she like both?" he asks puzzled.

"Maybe she just can't make up her mind. In Mitzi's defense, Koop could confuse the most rainbow flag–flying lesbian out there."

It was true. Koop was repulsive, arrogant, and just generally horrible, but his looks, charm, and money could blind almost any girl.

"Huh. So you think maybe this female lover had something to do with it?"

"I'm positive. This girl's been gunning for me ever since I got here. It's like she thinks I'm trying to replace Mitzi or something. I think she found out about Koop and just went into a rage. Let's face it, whatever happened to Mitzi was personal."

"I think you should get out of there, Aspen. Who's to say she won't do it again?" Harry asks, worried.

"No. I'm close, I can feel it. I just need to get into Cassandra's room and see if I can find some evidence."

"Aspen, you be careful. I'd never forgive myself if something happened to you," he says. I can tell by his voice how stressed he is. I know he wants to get me out of here but he also wants to find out what happened to his niece.

"This is a cake walk, Harry. Manis, pedis, and pizza parties twenty-four/seven," I lie. Someone bangs on the bathroom door startling me.

"Aspen, are you in there? I brought you back some steak," Charm yells.

"I'll be right there," I yell back. I flush the toilet to cover up my final words to Harry.

"I've gotta go. That's my roommate, Charm, calling for me," I tell him.

"What's she like?" he asks.

"She's the only normal one here," I say, clicking off.

❧

The next day on the way to class I feel like I could die from heat exhaustion. I am glad that I had thought to layer a Zeta tank top under my Zeta sweatshirt. I peel off the sweatshirt when I get to class. I look around for Grey but don't see her. Maybe the Zetas are actually starting to trust me and have called off the tail. Either that or they were busy going through my stuff back at the house. Thankfully I'd had the forethought to bring the locket and the note with me. After what happened yesterday, I know that things are getting serious now. I wasn't about to tell Harry about someone jacking me in the head because he would have pulled me out of the house faster than I could say, "GDI." I just need a little more evidence against Cassandra.

"Are you avoiding me?" a deep voice says, sliding into the seat next to me.

I look over to see Koop looking sort of unkempt for the first time ever. He's wearing cargo shorts and a T-shirt and his hair is absolutely gel-less. He still looks completely hot.

"Um, you're in my seat," Angel tells him, ready to dump her sugar-laden black coffee in his lap.

"Get another one," he says angrily.

"Koop, this is my friend, Angel. Angel, this is Koop," I say, making introductions before it gets ugly.

"What, I'm not your friend?" Koop says, displeased with the introduction. "If you're just going to blow me off then maybe I should just pull your little friend out of the test—"

"Koop, of course we're friends," I interrupt. The last thing I need is for Angel to know that I'm teaming up with Koop to help Tobi. She narrows her eyes at me and I know it's too late.

"I'll call you later," I tell him, covering his hand with mine. His eyes spark and I know I've pacified him for the time being. He throws Angel a dirty look before leaving the auditorium.

"Okay, what the hell is going on and why in God's name are you wearing a baseball hat?" she demands, taking her seat.

I take the hat off and turn so she can see the growth sticking out of the back of my head. She makes a squeaking noise and has her head buried in her hands sobbing when I turn back around.

"Oh my God, you've got a tumor. You're going to die, aren't you? And that guy is going to get you some drugs, right? But it's incurable, like Tobi, right?" she babbles on through sobs. I'm glad that she has taken to wearing less makeup or she would be covered in black eyeliner by now.

I consider agreeing with her assessment just to make my life easier for a few days, but I could never be that mean to Angel. Last year I could have let her think I was dying, no problem. Actually last year she would have been excited I was dying. But Angel is my friend now and that would be really wrong. Sometimes I can't believe how much I've matured.

"I'll tell you everything if you promise to keep it on the down low," I whisper. She wipes her eyes and nods. I gesture at her to leave the auditorium. There is no way I can take the chance of a Zeta mole overhearing all this top-secret information. We walk out of the auditorium together just as Professor Brown starts reminding us about how many people Ted Bundy fooled with his good looks and charm.

"So that's everything," I say after spilling my guts to Angel. She sits dazed, staring through all the sweaty bodies passing us on the quad.

"Do you really think Cassandra killed her?" she asks, amazed.

"It's the only thing that makes any sense. It had to be someone inside the house. The other sisters might even know about it and just aren't 'fessing up. They have this motto, "What happens at the Zeta house, stays at the Zeta house. They're all pretty off."

"What makes you think she won't kill you? She already did that to you," she says, pointing to my abnormally shaped head. "I don't think you should go back there," she says, worried.

"I have to just for a few days, just to get more on Cassandra. In the meantime, I need you to keep this stuff," I say, digging through my bag for the plastic bag containing the locket and note.

Angel takes it from me carefully and puts it in her bag.

"I don't like this, Aspen. Obviously Rand doesn't know any of this stuff. I know he'd never agree to you putting yourself in danger like this," she says.

"He knows the Cliffs Notes version. Besides, his head is so far up the Nus asses that he barely notices anything anymore," I say, rolling my eyes.

"It's just a stage," Angel says, sounding wise beyond her years. I laugh thinking how she was just doubting her own relationship a week ago.

"So what about the skull and crossbones guy?" she asks, referring to Koop.

"I've got to give him enough attention and information to keep him interested until Tobi gets better." I sigh, feeling exhausted. It is so tiring keeping all these balls in the air at once. I will totally need a vacation once this whole thing is over.

"God, could it be any hotter today?" Angel asks, pulling on her black shirt to get some air through it.

"I know, our weather is like so whacked," I agree, happy to be talking about the weather for once.

"Harry and Tobi are really lucky to have you for a friend," Angel says out of the blue.

"So are you," I remind her, getting a huge smile.

I skip the rest of my classes and head back to the sorority house. I'm almost there when my cell rings. It's Tobi. I find a bench on the quad and sit down just in case it's bad news.

"Hi, Tobi," I answer timidly.

"Aspen, this place is amazing. I'm staying in the most awesome condo right on the beach. All I do is swim and lay out all day. It's paradise," Tobi's ecstatic, healthy voice says.

I'm relieved that Koop obviously made sure that Tobi was treated like a VIP, but most of all I'm glad that Tobi is finally starting to sound like herself again.

"Are you going to be okay?" I ask.

"They say I'm as good as new. I just have to be observed some more. I don't know how you did this but I'm really glad you did." I can hear the smile in her voice.

Tobi and I say our good-byes and promise to meet up over Thanksgiving break. I hang up feeling good because I have one less ball to keep in the air: Koop. Although I'm sure he'd be happy with me juggling his balls as long as possible!

I walk the rest of the way to the house and sneak quietly inside, after unlocking all ten deadbolts. All of the sisters are gone. I don't know for how long but I know this might be my only opportunity to get into Cassandra's room.

I sneak back to the corridor behind the kitchen to Cassandra's room. As president she gets the biggest bedroom in the house, which happens to be on the main floor. I expect her to have a top of the line alarm system on her door so I'm surprised to find the door half open when I get there.

I peek around the door to make sure she isn't there. Satisfied that I'm alone, I creep in. It smells like bleach in here and everything looks so clean. I'm afraid to touch anything for fear of leaving fingerprints that wouldn't be visible to the naked eye but that Cassandra would surely be able to see. I don't even know what I'm looking for but the only thing that remotely has to do with Mitzi is a picture of her buried deep in Cassandra's desk drawer. I'm so aggravated that I don't even hear the footsteps until it's too late to hide.

"So I guess you know," Cassandra says, dropping her book bag to the floor.

Eleven

I could just kick myself for not sticking that jumbo can of pepper spray Harry gave me into my book bag. It would really come in handy when Cassandra starts trying to kill me. But she doesn't. She just sinks down onto her bed and starts to cry.

"I miss her so much," she says with a wail, throwing herself back into her pillows.

"Then why did you kill her?" I smart off, tired of playing games. She bolts upright in her bed, giving me a horrified look.

"How could you say such a thing? I loved Mitzi. I've been trying to figure out who could have done this." Tears flow from her huge eyes and puddle on her Zeta sweatshirt.

I know instantly that I'm not looking at a cold-blooded killer but a heartbroken girl.

"Why didn't you tell anybody about your relationship with Mitzi?"

"It's not like it would have helped solve the crime or anything. I didn't want her to be humiliated. She didn't want anybody to know. She didn't think her family would approve," she explains.

"Did you know she had a boyfriend?" I say. Cassandra's face registers pure shock then nothing but pain.

"She was cheating on me?" she whispers, taking it in. "Could he have killed her?" she says, suddenly whipping her head up.

"I really don't think so. I was convinced it was you. Now I don't have a clue who did this or why," I admit. I didn't want to alarm her and tell her that it had to be someone in the house because of my "accident" the other day. And considering the hardware the Zetas have on the front door I don't think anyone else is getting in.

"Are you going to tell?" she asks, looking pathetic while she dumps a puddle of antibacterial hand sanitizer in her palm. She rubs furiously until it disappears.

"No, there's no point." I suddenly add, "Why have you been so mean to me?"

She looks up in surprise, then shrugs. "I know who you are. The infamous Aspen Brooks. The super sleuth that took down the Beauty Bandit."

Now it's my turn to be surprised. "But how . . ."

"Mitzi used to tell me everything. She was really close to her uncle Harry and he used to brag about you all the time. Mitzi thought it was so cool you were able to crack the case before he did."

I instantly get warm fuzzies thinking about Harry bragging about me. He gives me a hard time but I know it's only because he cares about me.

"That still doesn't answer my question," I say.

"I knew that you would find out what really happened to her and I'm not sure I can handle knowing the truth," she admits.

I don't get people like Cassandra. I always have to know every tiny detail, no matter how gory. But maybe if something really horrible happened to Rand—I shudder at the thought—maybe I wouldn't want to know either.

"I don't have any idea what happened to her, Cassandra, and I'm not sure I ever will."

As irritating as it is, I have to admit, I don't have a clue where Mitzi is. But there is nothing I like better than a challenge.

"But I don't quit that easily," I tell her sternly.

"Yeah, I'm kind of getting that."

I turn to leave her room and she stops me.

"Aspen, our house really used to be a lot of fun. It just changed when Mitzi disappeared," she says.

It's hard to picture the Zeta house being like the Beta house but I smile and nod in agreement anyway.

@

Dinner with the sisters is like dining at a monastery. The only noises are Jocelyn sucking her thumb between bites and the sisters' forks clanking between bites of prime rib and cheese cubes. I am starting to crave an apple so bad that I feel possessed. I resolve to sneak out later to the farmers' market and gorge myself on fresh fruit.

I follow Charm back to our room and she immediately grabs her backpack to head to the library. I want to tell her about that study I heard about and that she isn't doing herself any favors by overstudying but I don't.

"I guess I'll see you tomorrow." I wave, depressed.

She stops, halfway out the door and asks, "What's wrong, Aspen?"

"You're gone all the time. I'm here all alone and the other sisters are just weird," I say, immediately covering my mouth when I realize what I've said. Charm is probably going to be so offended.

Instead she starts cracking up. She closes the door and sits down on her bed.

"Oh, they're all right, just a little misunderstood."

"Are you kidding me? You are the only normal one here. Well, besides me."

"I'm sorry I'm gone so much. It's just that this is my last semester and I really want to graduate with a four point zero grade point average. I've gotten straight As every semester and I don't want to blow it this semester."

"Wow, that's really an accomplishment." I don't envy all the time she spends in the library but it would be cool to have grades that good.

"There are definitely sacrifices you have to make for grades that good," she says, with a strange look on her face. If she means sacrificing time with the sisters, that's a sacrifice I can handle.

"You'll be pulling down a hundred grand a year when you get out of school," I tell her to which she grins devilishly.

"A girl can dream." She walks to the door and I realize that our quality time is over. It's back to the books for Charm.

I immediately call Rand when she leaves. I feel like I haven't talked to him, I mean, really talked to him, in weeks. It rolls to voice mail and I hang up before leaving a message. I'm sure he's off doing something with his brothers.

I click on the television and find one of those Lifetime movies that are like four hours long. I snuggle under my covers and lose myself in B-movie betrayal.

◎

I shouldn't have eaten all that prime rib and cheese. I'm going to be bound up until Thanksgiving and I'm dying of thirst. The clock next to my bed says it's twelve-thirty. I must have passed out somewhere during the second half of the movie.

Charm is sound asleep with her mouth hanging open, a delicate snore escaping it. Her ebony hair is tossed over her pillow and even snoring she looks like she should be wearing a tiara. I was so out of it I didn't even hear her come in.

I slip on some sweats and wrap a scrunchie around my hair, pulling it into a bun. I pad down the stairs hoping to avoid as many sisters as possible. My head hurts and I'm sick of this place. I'm surprised, but pleased, to find the house dark and all the sisters in their rooms.

In the kitchen I seek out the largest glass I can find. I find a plastic cup from a Zeta-Nu charity event last year that rivals the size of a Big Gulp. I fill it to the rim with ice-cold water from the dispenser and start chugging. I swear I'm not eating red meat for a year after leaving this place. I sit down at the tiny café table in the shadows of the kitchen and keep gulping. I'll probably be up half the night peeing but my fingers start to feel like fingers again instead of small sausages so it's all good.

I sit in the dark and wonder what Rand is doing. I miss him so much and I can't believe he didn't call me all day today. I have to make our relationship my number one priority after getting out of this house. I'm all for him making new friends and stuff but I'm not taking a back-seat to a bunch of dorky frat guys.

When I lower my glass I'm startled to see Lilly standing near the sliding-glass doors. I think this may be the
only time I've actually seen her conscious. She is looking
around suspiciously. She can't see me because I'm in the
shadows. I'm about to say something to her when she slips
out the door. I watch her quietly close the door and take
off across the back lawn, a tote bag flopping against her
side.

Something about the way she is acting makes me follow her. I slide on somebody's tennis shoes left at the back
door (so foul, but desperate times call for desperate mea-
sures) and head quietly out the back. She is already
headed around the front so I have to kick it in to catch up.
Once around the front of the house, she darts across the
quad. I'm careful to follow far enough behind so if Lilly
turns around I can duck behind a tree. I'm not positive,
but I don't think the sisters would be too happy if a new-
bie frog got busted tailing a senior. Luckily undercover
surveillance is totally my thing.

She starts leading me to a side of campus I've never
been to. The shops start looking grimy and most of the
fluorescent signs are missing almost all of their letters. She
turns and walks down a dark alley. I contemplate ditching
and heading back to the house, but now I've just got to
know where she's going. She always came off as very pure
and innocent, when she wasn't falling asleep, and for her
to be walking around in the middle of the night in the
seedy part of campus is fascinating enough for me to risk

my own neck. I do wish I had my cell with me though, or at the very least, my whistle.

She steps out of the alley, and knocks twice on an unmarked door that I wouldn't have even known was there. The door opens and she slides in before I can see anything. Shit. I head out of the alley and follow the sidewalk past the door and around to the front. The building is about a million years old with no windows in the front. A large stop sign is bolted to a thick concrete door announcing that this is the Bust Stop. It really irks me when people don't double-check their spelling. It's bus stop, people. Wait, the bus stop? Is Lilly taking off in the middle of the night without even saying good-bye or explaining her disappearance to the sisters? Could her disappearance have anything to do with Mitzi? This could be my last shot at actually getting some information and nothing is going to stop me.

I jog around to the back and knock twice on the door. A large, burly arm pulls me inside before I even realize the door has opened. I'm immediately on the defensive ready to give this guy a little of what I gave Koop the night he tried to scare me.

"You must be the new girl. It's nice to see somebody taking a little pride in her work and showing up prepared," a bald-headed, stocky man says, staring down at my chest. I so didn't need him pointing out that my chest was adapting to the sudden chill in the air in an embarrassing way. I immediately cross my arms over my chest to hide my girly parts.

"Awww . . . shucks. I thought maybe you'd like to give me a preview before going on for the first time," he says, finally meeting my eyes, and licking his chapped lips. I feel a strong urge to vomit prime rib on his filthy flip-flops, especially after seeing his toenails that haven't been trimmed in a decade.

"Stop talking to me like that. This is a public place and I have the right not to be verbally assaulted if I want to buy a bus ticket," I tell him sharply.

"Huh?" he asks confused, as he tosses me a tote bag.

"This is the bus stop, right?" I ask, looking around desperately for Lilly.

"It's pronounced Bust Stop, little lady." He laughs, as I start to feel incredibly naïve. "Now get these on and get out there and shake your little moneymaker." He swats my butt and I yelp. Does the owner here not give manda-tory sessions on sexual harassment in the workplace? It's outrageous.

I gather the tote and walk toward the only room I see. I've got to get out of here and figure I'll just sneak out the front instead of dealing with Casanova here again. What the hell is Lilly doing coming to a place like this?

I get my answer as soon as I enter the room. Girls are in various stage of undress all over the room. Feather boas, wigs, and pasties are flying everywhere. I stand star-ing like a fourteen-year-old boy, unable to believe my eyes. It's a strip club. Most of the girls look to be my age or younger. They are laughing and gossiping as they slide into their miniscule costumes, which, I've realized now, is why my tote bag is so light. I mean, how much could a couple of pasties and a thong weigh?

I spot Lilly sitting at a lighted vanity applying hooker red lipstick. I only know it's her because of her body badge. She looks amazing, in a totally slutty way, in her purple thong, pasties, and silver wig. I weave my way through the girls to get to her, getting sidetracked when I see a locker with Mitzi's name on it. Lilly exits through several strings of beads before I can reach her. I could yell but I don't really want to bring added attention to myself. I follow her out into a smoke-filled hallway. Raunchy hip-grinding music is blaring and I hear cries of dozens of drunken males.

" 'Scuse me, sweetie," somebody says from behind me. I move to the side without looking back. A shapely girl with blond pigtails on four-inch heels scoots around me. The hallway isn't big enough for both of us and her enormous rack grazes against my arm.

"I won't even charge you for that," she drawls sweetly. I don't say anything because I am just so in awe that she can actually stand upright with those things strapped to her chest.

"And now the moment you've all been waiting for, the Bust Stop's naughtiest school girl, Cheyenne," a skinny guy calls out over a microphone from a DJ booth in the corner of the club.

Little Miss Pigtails struts her stuff to the middle of the

stage and starts doing these elaborate gymnastic moves that leave me wondering how in the world that thong stays put. Men are throwing money all over the stage as Cheyenne gyrates in their direction. It's totally nauseating how guys act when they see a little skin. And the school-girl fantasy? Oh my God, so played out; the only thing Cheyenne would be using a book for is a doorstop.

I'm about to take my chances with the bald perv and sneak out the back when I see a familiar face. Again I'm hit with the sensation that I'm going to blow prime rib everywhere. Rand has a front row seat for Cheyenne's action. One glance tells me he's completely shit-faced. His Nu brothers, huddled around him, are whooping it up and throwing money toward the stage while he looks deep into his mug of beer for answers. I stand here frozen, not knowing what to do.

If I storm onstage and pull him home by his ear, Lilly will know I've seen her and she might clam up about Mitzi. I can't believe that Mitzi was moonlighting as a stripper. I can't help but wonder if maybe this place has something to do with her disappearance. It makes more sense than anything else. Aren't strip clubs usually owned by mobsters? Maybe Mitzi saw something she wasn't supposed to and they offed her. Although now that I think about it, I don't think central Illinois is a hotbed of mobster activity.

Soon Cheyenne's time onstage is over and Lilly comes strutting out. Several of the Nus are prodding Rand to look up and get more proactive in the whole experience. He doesn't look like he is particularly enjoying himself but I am still thoroughly pissed. Then I see him take out his wallet and remove some cash. He stands up and sticks it under Lilly's thong. I am positive my head is going to explode and I can't stop myself from storming across the stage.

"Rand Bachrach, what the hell are you doing?" I scream. I know I look like a crazy person in my Zeta sweats and bedhead, but I don't care. It's not even jealousy. I mean, what Rand and I have totally transcends a pair of pasties and a thong. It's the fact that he's giving into what these guys want so that they'll be his friends.

"Aspen?" Rand slurs in shock.

"Busted," a few of the Nus shout, laughing.

Lilly stops dancing and looks horrified to see me standing in front of her. "Aspen, I didn't know he was your boyfriend," she says guiltily.

"Lilly, we'll talk later," I tell her. She nods and gyrates across the room to take someone else's money.

"What are you doing here?" Rand asks me, rubbing his eyes hoping I'm just a mirage.

"That doesn't matter. I thought you were going to quit doing all this crap." I gesture at the beer mug in front of him.

"Are you gonna let her talk to you like that, Bachrach? I wouldn't put up with that from my bitch for a second," a smart-ass Nu says.

"The only bitch you could get is a female dog. This is

an A B conversation, now C your way out of it, loser," I tell him, my blood pressure going through the roof.

"You don't have to put up with this, Rand. There are a ton of women out there who aren't so high maintenance," the smart-ass says. No he didn't. I'm seriously about to knock this guy out.

"What do you care what I do? You're always off with Koop anyway. Don't try to deny that you aren't attracted to him!" Rand shouts back at me. I stand here in shock, not believing that he is still stuck on Koop. If he only knew what I really thought of Koop.

"She's a cheating slut, Rand. Kick her to the curb," a brother in the shadows says. They all start patting Rand on the back. He doesn't even bother to defend me. I think of how touching the scene between Angel and Lucas was the other day, so opposite of this moment. I feel like Rand is choosing these idiots over me. It is outrageous and I am furious. I really hate that it has come to this but I have no choice. Rand is just asking for it.

"You know what, Rand? You're acting like a real geek." I hate pulling that word out of my verbal arsenal but I have to snap some sense into Rand. His mouth falls open as I stomp off.

☺

I go back to the changing room where Lilly is waiting for me.

"Aspen," Lilly shouts, bouncing up tipsy on her heels. "You aren't going to tell the sisters, are you?" she pleads. "They'll strip me of my sisterhood," she continues before I can even comment.

We both start cracking up at the irony of her last statement. Tears start rolling down her cheeks and I'm quick to reassure her that I will keep her secret.

"Nobody is going to find out from me, but there were quite a few Nus out there and with that tattoo of yours, somebody will find out eventually," I say.

"Oh, yeah," she says, touching her lower back as if this thought hadn't occurred to her. She nods her head yes and I'm fairly certain she'll be covering her tattoo from now on.

"Besides, I totally get it. You need the money. You can probably make more here in one night than working two weeks somewhere else."

"Nah, I don't need the money. I just like it." she says, slipping out of her stilettos.

Um, okay.

"So what about Mitzi? Did she need the money?" I ask, pointing to the locker with her name on it.

Lilly looks confused as she looks to the locker. Then she shakes her head no.

"That's not the Zeta who disappeared. That's a different Mitzi. That's not even her real name."

I'm not sure if I am relieved or disappointed. I don't have to tell Harry that his niece stripped in her free time, which is good, but I also have to finally admit that I hadn't been able to solve her disappearance. Harry didn't know anything more than he had before I got here. I really hate it when things don't go the way I want them to.

The clock in the dressing room says it's three a.m. Lilly and I are both exhausted so we walk back to the house together in silence. Rand and his brothers were already gone when we left. Even though I am furious with him, I hope that he comes to his senses tomorrow when he sobers up.

We start to walk a little faster as the temperature drops even more. I can hardly believe I'd worn a tank top earlier today. Before Lilly slides the back door of the sorority house open, she turns to me as if to verify my secrecy. I don't say a word, but just pull an imaginary lock closed on my lips and throw away the key. She smiles and nods.

She heads upstairs while I slip off the borrowed tennis shoes. I tiptoe up the stairs and into my room. Charm is still in the same position as when I left but her snoring has gotten louder. She is about the only thing I am going to miss about this house and I'm not looking forward to saying good-bye to her tomorrow.

Twelve

I wake up in a panic, knowing immediately that I over-slept. I throw the sheets back and head for the bathroom, taking the fastest shower imaginable. While slipping into a Zeta tee and shorts, I hope that I have enough time to make it across campus to get to my literature test on time. My professor had already explained at the beginning of the semester that the only excuse to make up a test is death.

I don't bother blow-drying my hair, knowing that if the temperature is anything like it was yesterday it will dry quickly anyway. I skip putting on my makeup know-ing that I don't have time. Lucas's comment about letting myself go immediately comes to mind and I can't wait to get back to my normal life so I have plenty of time to primp.

I throw open the bathroom door to find Charm sitting in her bed surrounded by her books.

"What are you doing home?" I ask, puzzled. She is always gone way before I even get up.

She smiles and points to the window. I walk over and peer through the blinds. I'm blinded by whiteness. Snow. Tons of it.

"What the . . . ?" I say, shaking my head in confusion. Had I bumped my head harder than I thought? Had I been out for weeks? It is still October. We have wacky weather but this is crazy.

"Apparently it's some kind of record. They completely closed down the campus today, which has never been done. How cool is that?" She smiles. I'm sort of surprised that she is so psyched about it but then I remember her telling me about a test she is really nervous about. She's probably glad she's got more time to study.

"Everything is closed?" I ask, confused. Today is supposed to be my last day in the house but I can't very well go traipsing across campus with all my stuff in waist deep snow, especially when I don't even have my Uggs here. Freaking global warming! How in the world is a girl supposed to plan her wardrobe?

"The phones are out too," she adds, making my heart race. No phones? Trapped in the Zeta house with no way out for who knows how long? I feel myself start to panic.

"It'll be fun. Just a girls' day," she adds, burying her nose back in her book.

I lay down on my bed and try to get ahold of myself. It isn't the end of the world. I'll have more time to study for my lit test, which I need. It would be good for Rand not to be able to reach me for a while after last night and the only other person who seems to call lately is Koop and I don't want to talk to him anyway. Besides, I still have e-mail.

"No e-mail either. The house is still on dial-up," Charm says, reading my mind.

Dial-up? Who still uses dial-up? That's the equivalent of having one of those phones where you have to dial it by putting your finger in a hole and pulling it around. They are like so ancient that I don't even know the name. Like rotisserie or something.

Panic seizes my heart hard this time. What if Mitzi's killer really is in the house? I have to stop this. It is ridiculous. I've been in the house for weeks; one more day isn't going to kill me. I hope anyway. Then I remember my cell phone; surely it's not out too. I grab my purse and pull out my phone. I turn it on only to get the all-familiar angry beep telling me the battery is dead. I plug it into the charger knowing it's going to be a few hours just to get enough of a charge to make a short call. My phone and I have a hate-hate relationship.

I decide to venture out into the house for some breakfast. I am starving.

"Want some breakfast?" I ask Charm to which she

barely shakes no. So much for her being the entertainment committee today.

I plod down the hall toward the smell of bacon. I am craving a bowl of cereal so bad I'm about to freak out. I'm going on a serious carbohydrate binge when I get out of this place.

"Hey, Aspen," several sisters say as I enter the kitchen. Jocelyn holds her fingers in the air in a wave without removing her thumb from her mouth. Bowls of scrambled eggs mixed with some prime rib left over from last night litter the table. I'm suddenly not hungry and get myself a diet pop from the fridge.

"How weird is this weather?" Cassandra asks me brightly. I have to restrain myself from falling off my chair at her pleasant demeanor. She must think we are friends now that I've found her out. I look around the table but most of the sisters are chatting amongst themselves. Grey throws a wicked glance my way and I realize that I wasn't the only one to notice Cassandra's change of heart. I look away from her immediately and focus on Cassandra.

"Pretty weird. Charm said that phones and the Internet are out?" I ask, hoping she was wrong.

"Yep, luckily we still have electricity and plenty of food," she says, scooping herself a big portion of eggs. "I thought we could all watch some movies later," she says, happily.

I smile and nod. Maybe Cassandra isn't so bad after all. I guess she must have some redeeming qualities if Mitzi was with her. And the movies might be kind of fun; we haven't done anything like that since I got here. Maybe we'll do some sisterly bonding after all.

I thought Cassandra meant we would spend the afternoon giggling over *Mean Girls* or sobbing over *The Notebook*, not going cross-eyed reading subtitles off French films. I'm seriously going to hurt myself or someone else if I don't get away from these girls and it's only mid-afternoon. The snow is piling up so deep outside we can't even open the front door for fear of a mini-avalanche. I'm getting some serious cabin fever already. Why does my life always seem to end up like a Stephen King novel? Last year it was *Carrie*; this year is starting to shape up like *The Shining*.

"I'm going to go hang out in my room for a while," I tell no one in particular. Grey gives me a dirty look and no one else even looks up from the film. I plod through the house to my room wearing my favorite fluffy pink slippers. It makes me homesick just looking at them. I really wish that I could hear my mom's voice right now telling me that everything is going to be okay.

I know that life will go on fabulously as usual for me. Tobi is almost completely well now, according to her last checkup, and she may even be able to enroll at State next semester. Rand will realize how stupid he is being and we'll be the perfect couple again. But Harry still won't know what happened to his niece. It will drive him crazy for the rest of his life and that drives me crazy. If only I could have found something out for him.

I turn the knob to our bedroom and see Charm hunched over her desk, crying.

"Charm, what's wrong?" I ask, walking toward her. It's the first time I've seen her look even the tiniest bit disheveled. Her hair is pulled back in a ponytail and she's not wearing any makeup.

"I just can't get this stuff," she says, gesturing at an organic chemistry textbook. "I just know I'm going to flunk this class."

"Why don't you take a break? I read somewhere that it isn't good for you to study constantly. You have to let your brain rest and do other things."

She laughs, letting out a little snort. "Is that even true?" She wipes her face and closes her book.

"Yeah, I'm serious. If you try and download too much information at one time, you can burn up your hard drive," I say seriously.

"Oh, Aspen, I wish I could be as relaxed as you are. You always seem to just know everything is going to be all right," she says, gazing at me with envy.

I get this all the time. People just want to be me. I usually feel kind of bad for them but not Charm. Charm has everything going for her except that she seems to be a teensy bit neurotic about her grades.

"Why are you in this sorority?" I ask her, finally getting up the courage. I've been trying to figure it out since I got here. All the other girls are kind of dysfunctional and seem to need each other in a weird way, but not Charm.

"Because I know what it's like to be different," she answers, looking away. That's all she says and I'm not about to push my luck and ask her what she means. If she feels comfortable here, I guess that's all that matters. If there is one thing I've learned this semester, it's that people aren't always what they seem.

I pad over to my bed and decide to take a nap. If I am forced to be sequestered in this house of freaks then I'll just sleep through it. When I wake up, hopefully it will be ninety degrees out, and I can sneak out of here.

Charm cracks her book open again, completely disregarding what I just told her. Whatever! If she wants to fry her brain it isn't my business. I snuggle under my covers and start to drift away.

Someone pounds on our door nearly giving me heart failure. I bolt up in bed as Charm shouts, "Come in." Grey flings the door open looking flushed.

"Aspen, someone is here for you. It's a boy," she says, disgustedly. I flip the covers back and race down the hall. Standing in the foyer dressed in a snowsuit with a face mask pushed up to his forehead is Rand. I stop suddenly, glare at him, and jam my hands on my hips. So what if he trekked through a little snow? He is going to have to suck up big time for me to forgive him for all the stunts he's pulled the last few weeks.

"Hey, beautiful," he says in his adorable voice. I melt immediately like all the snow he's dragged in. I run over to him and wrap my arms around his neck, ecstatic to see him. Rand makes me feel safe, something I haven't felt since I moved into the Zeta house.

"I'm so sorry, Aspen. I didn't even want to go last night and I don't even like drinking. I'm gonna tell the guys I quit," he says, smoothing my hair back with his giant gloves.

"You don't have to quit. Just stop doing things you don't want to do," I tell him, kissing his frostbit lips.

"I've missed you, boo," he says, kissing me back. It dawns on me that we've attracted a crowd. I glance around at all the sisters watching us in awe, except Grey, who is seething.

"I thought there weren't supposed to be any boys in the house," Grey says to Cassandra.

"I think we can make an exception for love," she says, winking at me. I have to admit Cassandra has grown on me. I feel bad for her that she lost Mitzi. She was obviously in love with her. I smile back and hug Rand tightly. I lead him back to my room. Charm barely looks up from her book.

"Charm, this is my boyfriend, Rand," I say, helping Rand peel out of his snowsuit.

"Hi," Rand says, offering an ungloved hand. Charm looks up quickly and smiles then goes back to her book. Rand raises his eyebrows at me. We curl up together on my bed and start to fall asleep.

"What's that noise?" Rand asks. Scratching starts coming from above my bed and I realize we aren't the only ones snowed in.

"A family of squirrels has taken up residence in our attic. They drive me freaking crazy," I say, trying to ignore the scratching, which just makes me end up focusing on it.

Soon Rand is snoring lightly while I am still awake plotting painful deaths for the squirrels. I resolve to call my parents as soon as the phone lines are back up and make them take down the feeder in the front yard. Squirrels are not our friends. They can fend for themselves. *Scratch. Scratch.*

"Aspen, you have another visitor," Grey screams through the door. I sit up and head toward the door, leaving Rand sleeping. Charm throws me a dirty look. I shrug it off. It's not like I can help it that so many people love me.

"Oh, no. You're not staying here," I tell Koop, who is standing soaking wet in our foyer. "How did you even get here?" I understood how Rand had made it over just from the Nu house in back but Koop lived all the way across campus.

"I bribed the dorm maintainence man to use his Bobcat. I had to see you," he says desperately.

Besides the fact that he totally gets on my nerves, it is dangerous for him to be here. What if a sister recognizes him and puts it together he was with Mitzi then figures out what I'm really doing here. The last thing I need is to be found out the night before I blow this Popsicle stand.

"I'm sorry you came all this way. I don't have any new notes for you," I tell him, giving him an evil stare. All of the sisters are lining the staircase listening eagerly.

"What the hell is he doing here?" Rand yells, coming out of the hallway.

"He's leaving," I say, looking at Rand and raising an eyebrow. He knows immediately that I need him to play it cool.

"I'm not going anywhere," Koop says, kicking off his boots. "I'm in love with you, Aspen, and we're going to be together."

I drop my head into my hands and groan. I so knew this was going to happen. Koop is vulnerable missing Mitzi and I'm quite the package—how could he not transfer his Mitzi feelings to me? It is a classic case of transference. I learned that in Abnormal Psych.

"Aspen, maybe you should take this in your room," Cassandra offers. I lead the way to my bedroom and fling open the door. Charm takes one look at me and the two guys behind me and cracks up.

"Would you mind studying somewhere else for a little while?" I ask her, cringing. She shrugs like it's no big deal.

"I can't concentrate anyway," she says, glancing up.

"Thanks, I really appreciate it," I tell her, shutting the door behind her.

"You, sit, and you, sit," I order Rand and Koop pointing to opposite beds.

"I'm not in love with you and I never will be," I tell Koop. His sharp features drop, and for a second, I think he might cry.

"I'm not in love with him. I'm in love with you," I tell Rand, winking at him.

"Listen, Koop, I haven't found out anything about Mitzi. She's gone and she's never coming back. I don't think she was the person you thought she was anyway, so you need to get over her. I really appreciate you helping Tobi but I'm leaving the Zeta house tomorrow. So after today we really don't need to talk to each other again," I tell him.

"That's not acceptable. I always get what I want," he says, glaring at Rand. For a split second, I wonder if I could have been wrong about Koop. Could he have done something to Mitzi after all and this is an elaborate cover-up?

No, I have to stop thinking like this. Like everybody is a suspect. It's over and I have to stop driving myself crazy with it. *Scratch. Scratch. Scratch.* Those freaking squirrels have got a death wish, I swear.

"Not this time, Koop," I tell him sternly. Rand sits quietly on the bed listening to us. I love that even though we've been through a rough patch lately, he still knows that everything is going to be all right. I don't have to sit here and coddle him. He is just so mature. Well, except that crap he pulled last night!

"Dude, you need to move on," Rand says, very immaturely. I cringe knowing this isn't going to be good. Koop narrows his piercing green eyes at Rand.

"Dude, you need to fuck off," Koop replies. "Aspen has been on my jock since I got here. You were too busy with your brothers so I had to take care of her for you," he says, laughing evilly.

Rand leaps off the bed and tackles Koop. They drop to the floor punching each other.

"Stop it," I scream. "Rand, he's lying."

Our door flies open and the sisters watch in awe as Rand and Koop take turns bashing each other's brains out. I'm not about to get in the middle of those flying fists and risk damaging any of my facial features. I run over to my desk and scoop up my purse. I tip it over and dump out the contents. The jumbo bottle of pepper spray that Harry gave me falls out. I uncap the lid and walk over to Koop and Rand.

"This is your last warning. Stop fighting or you're going to be sorry," I warn them, shaking up the can. Fists, and now blood, are flying everywhere and it is beyond foul. I aim the nozzle toward them and spray. They break away from each other, spitting, with tears flowing from their eyes.

"Jesus, Aspen," Rand shouts at me through tears.

"You're a crazy bitch," Koop hollers between coughs, "that's why I love you."

The sisters are clapping like they are watching a choreographed skit. I back away from the fumes, knowing how detrimental they could be with my asthma. I know I shouldn't have sprayed the guys but everyone is just driving me crazy. I just want a little peace. I plop down onto my bed and try to take some deep breaths to calm myself. I just want my life back. It was bad enough that I didn't get into a cool sorority but now I have some psycho trust-fund baby stalker after me for who knows how long. A big part of me just wants to go back home where things are familiar, where I feel safe, where things aren't so crazy.

Even through Koop's coughing and Rand's complaining, I can hear the scratching start up again. I can't take it anymore. I shake the can of pepper spray and feel that I still have several more shots left. Those squirrels are going to pay. I may not be able to find Mitzi, stop Koop from torturing me and Rand, or get into Beta, but I can take care of these squirrels who have been begging for a confrontation since I got here.

"Somebody tell me how to get to the attic," I demand, glancing at the crowd of sisters gathered in the doorway.

Jocelyn pops her thumb out of her mouth and points down the hall. I run out of the room shaking the can of pepper spray.

"Aspen, where are you going?" Rand shouts behind me. I run down the hall and grab a cord I see hanging down. I pull down a set of stairs that fold out from the ceiling. Loud banging comes from the front door interrupting me. I peek around the stairs and over the balcony. The door busts open and a mountain of snow comes pouring in. A large person covered head to toe in ski gear barrels in followed by several other people in ski gear. The first person pulls off his ski mask and it's Harry. Harry and the entire campus police department.

"What are you doing?" I shout.

"Aspen, stay where you are," he demands, as he starts ordering people through the house.

"Look what you've done. This place is a mess," Cassandra screams at him while trying to clean up all the snow they've tracked in.

"Hi, what's your name?" Lucy practically purrs, winding herself around Harry.

"Aspen, come away with me," Koop pleads, suddenly at my side.

"Get away from her," a bloody Rand yells to an even bloodier Koop. They face off and start throwing punches again.

"Security breached, security breached," Grey screams about five minutes too late while Jocelyn stands next to her, unruffled, sucking her thumb.

"I can't take this anymore. You're all completely

twisted," I scream at the top of my lungs. Everyone freezes and their eyes are on me. For a split second it is absolutely still and then the scratching starts again.

"I've got some business to attend to," I yell, starting up the stairs. I may not be able to spray everyone downstairs but there is no way I'm leaving this house without giving these squirrels a piece of my mind. They've been testing me since I got here. I tiptoe up the steps while shaking the can. They are going to get the sneak attack of their lives.

It's pitch black up here except for a shadow I can see coming from a far corner of the attic. It almost looks like a television screen flickering. It goes out completely plunging me into darkness. I hear the scratching and rush ahead while holding the nozzle down.

"Take that you filthy vermin," I shout, filling the attic with pepper spray.

A bright light flickers on again and I'm close enough now that I can see. But instead of a family of rabid squirrels, I see a girl tied to a chair with duct tape across her mouth. I start coughing and my eyes are watering as I get closer. Even with tears pouring from her eyes I can see that it's Mitzi. She's been above me the whole time. I rip the tape off her mouth and try to scoot her chair over to the attic opening but my lungs are closing up from the pepper spray.

Why did I have to go so ballistic and use the whole can?

"I'll be right back," I tell her, coughing, trying to make my way out of the attic. I'm too weak to make it out. I collapse on the floor just as Harry comes bounding up. He scoops me up and takes me down the stairs.

"I found her for you, Harry," I tell him before passing out.

Thirteen

"Oh my God, not again!" I scream, sitting straight up in the hospital bed. Concerned faces of all the people who love me come into focus.

"Sweetheart, are you all right?" Mom asks, gently taking my hand, which has an IV poking out of it.

I fall back against the pillows, shaking my head no. Nothing is all right. Why can't they see that? No one understands what I'm going through. The crowd parts and I see Rand smiling down at me.

"It's the gown, isn't it, Aspen?" Rand asks. My eyes light up and I realize that someone *does* understand. Rand knows that after weeks of wearing nothing but sweat suits my body cannot possibly be subjected to a poly-cotton-whatever-blend, one-size-fits-all, butt-flashing gown.

My body will go into some sort of a fashion coma if I have to continue wearing this even one more second.

"I brought these for you." He grins, holding up my favorite pair of Karen Neuburger pajamas.

"I love you so much," I tell him weakly in a strange voice. I put my hand to my scratchy throat and realize Rand had to watch medics work some *ER* magic on me for the second time in our short courtship.

"Don't you ever scare me like that again, boo," he says, leaning down to kiss me.

"Jesus, get a room," Angel smarts off. I look over at her, dressed head to toe in Gore-Tex, and smile. Slowly everyone else comes into focus. Mom, Dad, Angel, Lucas, Koop, Cassandra, Charm, Harry, and Mitzi. Wait a minute, Mitzi?

Then I remember. I found her. I found Mitzi. I stormed up to the attic to off some squirrels and pepper sprayed Mitzi and myself.

"Are you okay?" I ask her. She looks okay, except for some chafed skin where the duct tape was, but I've got some kick ass concealer that I can loan her to take care of that. Actually she looks remarkably good, now that I think about it, to have lost all the blood that they found in her bed. Weird, I guess she's all healed up.

"You upstaged me again, Aspen Brooks," Harry says smiling.

"Does this mean you'll make me an honorary deputy? A badge would be the coolest accessory ever!" Everyone laughs and relaxes a little knowing I'm back to my old self.

"So what happened? Who kidnapped you, Mitzi?" I ask her. Her eyes dart to the floor and she doesn't answer.

"She never saw the person who kidnapped her. They took her to the attic and everyday someone would come up and leave her food and let her use the restroom but they were always disguised. None of the sisters saw anything," Harry explains.

"Why didn't they find her when they searched the sorority house?" I ask, confused.

Harry rolls his eyes. "Apparently the sisters were having a pillow fight in their panties and the guys were sort of distracted." Everyone in the room starts cracking up. Those Zetas are some twisted sisters!

"But what would someone get out of doing that? Just keeping her tied up?" I wonder aloud. It doesn't make any sense. Harry shrugs in confusion. He gazes over at his niece and beams with happiness. I don't really think he cares; he's just glad she's back. I guess it doesn't really matter who did it now that Mitzi's safe and I'm out of the house. My eyes find Koop's. I just realized that he is standing on the opposite side of the room as Mitzi.

"Koop, you've got her back. The love of your life," I say, excited. I feel like I'm happier than he is just because I know he won't be bugging me anymore. Rand starts to snicker and Koop throws him a dirty look.

"What's so funny?" I ask, confused.

"Tell her, Casanova," Rand says to Koop.

"I never actually dated Mitzi," Koop confesses, looking embarrassed.

"What do you mean? How could you have known all that stuff about her?" I ask, confused. Granted, most of the stuff he knew was wrong, but still. Wait a minute.

"You lied about everything, didn't you?" I yell at him, hurting my throat.

"I only did it so we could spend more time together. I knew eventually you would see that we belong together," Koop explains while rushing to my bedside.

"Dude, you are seriously pushing it," Rand says, pushing Koop away from me. Harry steps between them to curtail any more bloodshed.

"But what about the bracelet?" I ask, still reeling that I hadn't been able to see through Koop's lies. Was I slipping? Nah, surely not, Koop is just really good.

"It was just an expensive prop. My dad is one of Tiffany and Co.'s biggest customers. They had it delivered to me within hours," he replies smugly. "Of course you found it before you were supposed to but it ended up working out even better that way," he says, all cocky. I swear if I didn't have this IV in my strong arm, I'd punch him in his pearly whites. I can't believe I ever gave him the benefit of the doubt. Under his Tommy clothes, hair gel, and intoxicating cologne, he's nothing but a monster. I had him pegged right the second I met him. Note to self: Never, ever, doubt my first impression of people.

"Aspen, we're exactly alike. You know that we belong together," he says, leaning around Harry to flash me his gorgeous green eyes.

"No means no, Romeo," I say, giving Harry a look. He gets it and strong-arms Koop out of my room. We can still hear him screaming that he loves me halfway down the hall. I'm pretty sure I haven't seen the last of him but at least he's gone for tonight.

"Wait, so why were you busting into the house?" I ask, confused.

"I called him about your little 'accident,'" Angel says with air quotes. "You were getting in over your head, Brooks." She laughs hysterically at her own pun. I flip her off.

"What's she talking about, Aspen?" Rand asks, concerned.

"Somebody whacked her in the head and knocked her out the other day when she started getting too close to the truth," Angel interrupts. Lucas stays quiet and smiles gently at me.

"You should have told me, Aspen," Harry scolds me. My parents don't say a word but their eyes tell me a lecture is in my near future. Damn that Angel Ives.

"Everybody needs to ease up off me. I can't think in this gown. I need to change," I say, lifting myself out of bed very carefully so that I don't flash anybody. Mom pulls the curtain around my bed while I slip into the jammies that Rand so thoughtfully brought.

"You have to stop putting yourself in danger, Aspen," Mom says, worriedly.

"I didn't mean to worry you, Mom, but I had the perfect opportunity to help Harry and Tobi. I just had to take it," I tell her, climbing back into bed. I can't even imagine how bad my makeup and hair look but I'm too exhausted to care. These people have all seen me at my best and worst and they still love me.

"You sacrificed your own happiness to help Harry and Tobi?" Mom asks, surprised.

"Of course, they're my friends. I'd do anything for my friends," I tell her pulling the covers around myself.

"My little girl is all grown up," Mom says, dabbing at the tears suddenly in her eyes. She pulls the curtain back and everyone is standing with their mouths wide open except for Rand. They obviously overheard our whole conversation and are amazed that I would be so selfless, but not Rand. Rand knows there isn't anything I wouldn't do for the people I love. He moves over to my bed and kisses me with every fiber in his body.

"I think we'll go down to the cafeteria and grab some coffee," Dad says, ushering Mom out the door. I guess Dad still isn't comfortable seeing just how grown up I really am.

"Yeah, we better jet. It's still really bad out and it'll take forever to get back to the Beta house," Angel says, bear-hugging Lucas. "There's just one last thing: The Betas wanted me to give this to you," she says, holding out a gold pin identical to the one she has been wearing since she joined the Beta house.

"Wait. What?" I ask, confused.

"You should have been a Beta girl all along. The Betas think it's super cool what you did and they hope you'll consider being a sister." She leans down and kisses my forehead, which for some strange reason almost makes me cry. "I get it if you've had enough of the Greek life. I'll consider you a sister and best friend no matter what anyway," she says, a tear slipping down her cheek. I pull her into a big hug. I realize now how scared she must have been for me. I would have busted down the Betas' door if our roles had been reversed. She did the right thing by calling Harry.

As twisted as some of the Zetas are, I know that not all Greeks are like them. The Betas are a fun-loving, loyal, philanthropic bunch of girls, and I would love to be a part of their sorority.

"I've said it before, but I'll say it again. You're a good friend, Angel Ives, and I'd love to be your sister." I let go of her. She bounces up and down with excitement before waving and disappearing out of the room with Lucas's arm around her Gore-Tex–padded shoulders.

"I guess that leaves us," Harry says, awkwardly, turning to look at Mitzi. I think girlfriend is going to have some serious issues about being locked in an attic for a couple of months and Harry doesn't know where to start. It probably doesn't help matters that her kidnapper is still running free.

"Thanks for trying to save the day," I tease him. He leans in for a hug and squeezes extra hard. Mitzi is lucky to have such a great uncle. Harry is like me and he would do anything for the people he loves. It's probably killing him that he can't catch Mitzi's kidnapper and help ease her pain.

Who in the world would kidnap a girl just to keep her tied up? There was never a ransom and she was never hurt. Why would someone want people to think she was dead and how could they pull it off if she wasn't even hurt?

Professor Brown's lecture about Ted Bundy flashes in my mind. I remember him saying how normal Ted was and how he was living a successful life before he was arrested. Too bad none of the Zeta sisters were normal, that ruled them out, except for Charm, who was the only normal one, except for that teensy addiction to studying.

I look up at her and smile. She is the only sister who doesn't have some weird social defect. She seems to lead a very normal life. My head starts spinning with images and I rest my head against the pillow. I feel dizzy.

"Aspen, are you all right?" Rand asks, concerned.

Images of Charm buried in her books spin through my head. Charm saying she knew what it was like to be different. Charm crying because she thought she might be getting a B in organic chemistry. Charm volunteering at the blood drive where Mitzi regularly gave blood. Charm hauling around a backpack so heavy it could be registered as a lethal weapon. I rub the bump still protruding from the back of my head and just know that damn backpack was the cause.

"It was you, wasn't it?" I say, staring straight at Charm. Harry and everyone else spin around taking in Charm's guilty expression.

"You wanted it to look like Mitzi was dead so the school would give you straight As, didn't you?" I continue, sitting up. Charm's eyes well up with tears as she nods her head yes. I can't believe I hadn't thought of it before. It makes perfect sense.

"I'll be damned," Harry says, stunned, removing a pair of handcuffs from his belt loop.

"You kept me locked in the attic all that time? You?" Mitzi yells in Charm's face. "We were friends. We were roommates. Who does that to a person?"

"I'm really sorry, Mitzi. I was getting a C. I can't get a C," Charm explains, hanging her head.

"I hate you," Mitzi screams then slaps Charm across the face. Harry looks around in panic, probably worried about being accused of letting his niece get some street justice with her attacker. Rand and I look around the room and start whistling like we didn't see a thing.

"Come on, let's go get you your own nice little cell so you can study as much as you want." Harry laughs, leading a handcuffed Charm out of the room.

"Hey, Malone, you owe me big time," I shout after him. He pops his head back into the room and winks at me.

"Don't I know it." He holds out a hand and pretends to tremble.

"I'll be around to collect when you least expect it," I say, laughing. He blows me a kiss then disappears out the door.

"Thanks for everything, Aspen," Mitzi says, starting for the door. Cassandra trails her, unable to take her eyes off Mitzi.

"Hey, Mitzi, why did you join the Zetas?" I ask, nervous to hear the answer.

"I had seen Cassandra in her letters around campus and I wanted to get to know her. So I rushed. The rest is history." She smiles at me.

"I never knew that," Cassandra tells her as they wave to me and disappear into the hall.

"Thank goodness. That means Mitzi's normal," I tell Rand.

"You did it again, boo," Rand says.

"What? Saved the day?" I laugh.

"Yep. You are turning into quite the little detective," he says, pulling a chair bedside my bed. I nod happily in agreement. By the time I get out of college my resume is going to be so jam-packed full of mysteries I've solved and people forever indebted to me, I'll be able to write my own ticket.

"What are you doing?" I ask.

"I'm not leaving your side," he says sweetly.

"Duh, I know that. I meant why aren't you in bed with me?"

He smiles mischievously, slips off his coat and shoes and climbs into the tiny hospital bed with me. He begins softly stroking my hair, which he knows I love.

"I'm ready for spring break," I tell him, sighing with exhaustion. Between rushing, classes, and solving Mitzi's disappearance, I'm ready for some fun in the sun. Unfortunately spring break is still about five months away.

"I'll take you somewhere tropical, anywhere you want to go, I promise," he says, lightly kissing my neck.

"The Bahamas?" I ask, imagining walking hand in hand on the pure white sand with Rand.

"Ooh, yeah. Paradise Island. Do you want me to tell you a story?" he whispers in my ear. I nod. Rand tells the best stories ever.

"You and I have our own cabana right by the ocean. The temperature is just right and when you get too hot I spritz you down with Evian. The waves are crashing onshore and the water is so clear you can see down for miles. We have our own personal butler who brings us tropical drinks, nonalcoholic, of course." He laughs.

I close my eyes and start to drift away imagining Rand's story. I'm almost asleep when I jerk myself back to consciousness.

"Rand?"

"Yes, Aspen," he whispers.

"What am I wearing?"

Top Ten Reasons I'm Attending College

BY ASPEN BROOKS

10) I so don't do hairnets, and working around French fry grease would totally ruin my complexion, so working fast food is out.

9) Dorm food really isn't that bad.

8) Excuse to buy new color-coordinated school supplies.

7) I look really good in State University's colors.

6) I love my folks but a girl's gotta cut the cord sometime.

5) Because Harry is paying for it!

4) Sororities kind of frown on girls rushing who don't attend college there.

3) You have to be twenty-one before you can apply for *The Apprentice*.

2) Rand is going! Aspen hearts Rand! Aspen-n-Rand forever!

And the number one reason is:

1) To get smarter because everybody knows that smart chicks rock!

Berkley Jam
delivers the drama

Rich Girl: A BFF Novel
by Carol Culver

A new semester is beginning at Manderley Prep,
where being wealthy doesn't make you popular—
but it certainly opens doors...

Not Anything
by Carmen Rodrigues

After her mother's death, Susie Shannon closed herself
off from the world—until Danny Diaz helps her open
her heart again.

Violet by Design
by Melissa Walker

The lure of international travel draws Violet back into
the glamorous world of medeling, and all the drama it
brings with it.

Go to penguin.com to order!